He stared at her for a long moment, taking in the parted lips, the glittering eyes...an expression he knew all too well. He lowered his head, and an inner shout of exultation went off in his skull when she didn't flinch away but met him halfway.

Their lips connected and it was as if a match had been struck in the presence of gasoline fumes. They both went up in flames.

A low moan slid between them. One that most certainly hadn't come from him. Taking that as a signal to continue, he lifted his fingers and tunnelled deep into her hair, the damp moisture of her scalp feeling cool against his overheated skin.

Ignoring the microscope and slides, he shifted her legs sideways until they rested between his, without breaking contact with her mouth for even a second.

The change in position pressed her thigh against his already tightening flesh, which was pure torture—it made him want to push back to increase the contact. He forced himself to remain still instead, although it just about killed him. It had been four years since he'd held this woman in his arms, and he wasn't about to blow it by doing anything that would have her leaping from his lap in a panic. Realistically he knew they weren't going to have sex here, but he could take a minute or two to drink his fill of her.

Only he'd never really get his fill. Would always want more than she was willing to give.

Dear Reader

There comes a time in our lives when we're confronted with tough challenges or painful decisions. When those decisions are of a life-changing nature there's a temptation to draw inward and isolate ourselves, locking out those who love us the most.

Tracy Hinton faces just such a situation. And at a time when she should lean on her husband the most she shuts him out completely, creating a rift that soon grows too wide to bridge.

That could have been the end of the story, but sometimes we're given a second chance—an opportunity to right the wrongs of the past. What we do with that chance will set the course for our future. Will we waste it? Or will we embrace it and accept the good things life has to offer?

Thank you for joining Ben and Tracy as they embark on a very special journey of healing and second chances. In confronting the mistakes of the past they rekindle a love that has never quite died. These two characters stayed with me long after I wrote 'The End'. I hope you enjoy reading their story as much as I enjoyed writing it.

Love

Tina Beckett

HER
HARD TO RESIST
HUSBAND

BY
TINA BECKETT

Published in Great Britain 2014
by Mills & Boon, an imprint of Harlequin (UK) Limited,
Eton House, 18-24 Paradise Road, Richmond, Surrey, TW9 1SR

© 2014 Tina Beckett

ISBN: 978 0 263 24158 7

Harlequin (UK) Limited's policy is to use papers that are natural,
renewable and recyclable products and made from wood grown in
sustainable forests. The logging and manufacturing processes conform
to the legal environmental regulations of the country of origin.

Printed and bound in Great Britain
by CPI Antony Rowe, Chippenham, Wiltshire

Born to a family that was always on the move, **Tina Beckett** learned to pack a suitcase almost before she knew how to tie her shoes. Fortunately she met a man who also loved to travel, and she snapped him right up. Married for over twenty years, Tina has three wonderful children and has lived in gorgeous places such as Portugal and Brazil.

Living where English reading material is difficult to find has its drawbacks, however. Tina had to come up with creative ways to satisfy her love for romance novels, so she picked up her pen and tried writing one. After her tenth book she realised she was hooked. She was officially a writer.

A three-times Golden Heart finalist, and fluent in Portuguese, Tina now divides her time between the United States and Brazil. She loves to use exotic locales as the backdrop for many of her stories. When she's not writing you can find her either on horseback or soldering stained glass panels for her home.

Tina loves to hear from readers. You can contact her through her website or 'friend' her on Facebook.

Recent titles by the same author:

THE LONE WOLF'S CRAVING**
NYC ANGELS: FLIRTING WITH DANGER*
ONE NIGHT THAT CHANGED EVERYTHING
THE MAN WHO WOULDN'T MARRY
DOCTOR'S MILE-HIGH FLING
DOCTOR'S GUIDE TO DATING IN THE JUNGLE

NYC Angels
**Men of Honour duet with Anne Fraser*

To my husband, who stands beside me
through thick and thin.

And to my editor, Suzy,
for making me dig deeper than I ever thought I could.

CHAPTER ONE

TRACY HINTON DIDN'T faint.

Her stomach squirmed and threatened to give way as the scent of death flooded her nostrils, but she somehow held it together. Calming herself with slow, controlled breaths was out of the question, because breathing was the last thing she wanted to do right now.

"How many are there?" She fitted the protective mask over her nose and mouth.

"Six deaths so far, but most of the town is affected." Pedro, one of her mobile clinic workers, nodded towards the simple clay-brick house to his left, where an eerily still figure was curled in a fetal position on the porch. Another body lay a few yards away on the ground. "They've been dead for a few days. Whatever it was, it hit fast. They didn't even try to make it to a hospital."

"They were probably too sick. Besides, the nearest hospital is twenty miles away."

Piauí, one of the poorest of the Brazilian states, was more vulnerable to catastrophic infections than the wealthier regions, and many of these outlying townships relied on bicycles or their own two feet for transportation. It was hard enough to make a twenty-mile trek even when one was young and healthy, which these poor souls had not been. And cars were a luxury most couldn't afford.

She wouldn't know for sure what had caused the deaths

until she examined the bodies and gathered some specimens. The nearest diagnostic hospital was a good hundred miles from here. In any case, she'd have to report the possibility of an epidemic to the proper authorities.

Which meant she'd have to deal with Ben.

Pedro shook his head. "Dengue, you think?"

"Not this time. There's some blood on the front of the man's shirt, but nothing else that I can see from this distance." She stared at the crude corral where several pigs squealed out a protest at the lack of food. "I'm thinking lepto."

Pedro frowned. "Leptospirosis? Rainy season's already over."

The area around the house consisted of a few desiccated twigs and hard-packed clay, confirming her colleague's words. The sweltering heat sucked any remaining moisture from the air and squeezed around her, making her nausea that much worse. Situated close to the equator, the temperature of this part of Brazil rarely dipped below the hundred-degree mark during the dry season. The deadly heat would only grow worse, until the rains finally returned.

"They have pigs." She used her forearm to push sticky tendrils of hair from her forehead.

"I saw that, but lepto doesn't normally cause hemorrhaging."

"It did in *Bahia*."

Pedro's brows went up. "You think it's the pulmonary version?"

"I don't know. Maybe."

"Do you want to take samples? Or head for one of the other houses?"

Reaching into the back pocket of her jeans, she eased out her cellphone and glanced hopefully at the display. No bars. What worked in São Paulo obviously didn't work here. "Is your phone working?"

"Nope."

She sighed, trying to figure out what to do. "The tissue samples will have to wait until we come back, I don't want to risk contaminating any live patients. And maybe we'll come within range of a cellphone tower once we hit higher ground."

Benjamin Almeida pressed his eye to the lens of the microscope and twisted the fine focus until the image sharpened, making the pink stain clearly visible. Gram negative bacteria. Removing the slide, he ran it through the digital microscope and recorded the results.

"Um, Ben?" His assistant's hesitant voice came from the doorway.

He held up a finger as he waited for the computer to signal it had sent his report to the attending physician at the tropical disease institute of *Piauí*. The man's office was fifteen steps away in the main hospital building, but Ben couldn't take the time to walk over there right now. Dragging the latex gloves from his hands and flicking them into the garbage can to his right, he reached for the hand sanitizer and squirted a generous amount onto his palm.

"Yep, what is it?" He glanced up, his twelve-hour shift beginning to catch up with him. There were two more slides he needed to process before he could call it a day.

"Someone's here to see you." Mandy shifted out of the doorway, the apology in her cultured Portuguese tones unmistakable.

"If it's Dr. Mendosa, tell him I just emailed the report. It's a bacterial infection, not a parasite."

A woman appeared next to Mandy, and Ben couldn't stop his quick intake of breath. Shock wheeled through him, and he forced himself to remain seated on his stool, thankful his legs weren't in charge of supporting his weight at that moment.

Inky-dark hair, pulled back in its usual clip, exposed high cheekbones and a long slender neck. Green eyes—right now filled with worry—met his without hesitation, her chin tilting slightly higher as they stared at each other.

What the hell was *she* doing here?

The newcomer adjusted the strap of a blue insulated bag on her shoulder and took a small step closer. "Ben, I need your help."

His jaw tensed. Those were almost the exact words she'd used four years ago. Right before she'd walked out of his life. He gave a quick swallow, hoping his voice wouldn't betray his thoughts. "With what?"

"Something's happening in São João dos Rios." She patted the bag at her side, words tumbling out at breakneck speed. "I brought samples I need you to analyze. The sooner the better, because I have to know why people are suddenly—"

"Slow down. I have no idea what you're talking about."

She bit her lip, and he watched her try to collect her thoughts. "There's an outbreak in São João dos Rios. Six people are dead so far. The military police are already on their way to lock down the town." She held her hand out. "I wouldn't have come if this wasn't important. Really important."

That much he knew was true. The last time he'd seen her, she had been heading out the door of their house, never to return.

He shouldn't be surprised she was still roving the country, stamping out infectious fires wherever she went. Nothing had been able to stop her. Not him. Not the thought of a home and family. Not the life she'd carried inside her.

Against his better judgement, he yanked on a fresh pair of gloves. "Do I need a respirator?"

"I don't think so. We used surgical masks to collect the samples."

He nodded, pulling one on and handing another to her, grateful that its presence would hide those soft pink lips he'd never tired of kissing. Ben's attention swiveled back to her eyes, and he cursed the fact that the vivid green still had the power to make his pulse pound in his chest even after all this time.

He cleared his throat. "Symptoms?"

"The commonality seems to be pulmonary hemorrhage, maybe from some type of pneumonia." She passed him the bag. "The bodies have already been cremated, unfortunately."

"Without autopsies?" Something in his stomach twisted in warning.

"The military let me collect a few samples before they carted the bodies away, and the government took another set to do its own studies. I have to document that I've destroyed everything once you're done." She lowered her voice. "There's a guard in your reception area whose job it is to make sure that order is carried out. Help me out here. You're the best epidemiologist around these parts."

He glanced at the doorway, noting for the first time the armed member of the *Polícia Militar* leaning against the wall in the other room. "That wasn't one of my most endearing features, once upon a time."

He remembered all too well the heated arguments they'd had over which was more important: individual rights or the public good.

Biting her lip, she hesitated. "Because you went behind my back and used your job as a weapon against me."

Yes, he had. And not even that had stopped her.

His assistant, who'd been watching from the doorway, pulled on a mask and moved to stand beside him, her head tilting as she glanced nervously at the guard. Her English wasn't the best, and Ben wasn't sure how much of their conversation she'd grasped. "Is he going to let us leave?" she asked in Portuguese.

Tracy switched to the native language. "If it turns out the illness is just a common strain of pneumonia, it won't be a problem."

"And if it isn't?"

Ben's lips compressed as he contemplated spending an unknown amount of time confined to his tiny office.

With Tracy.

He had a foldable cot in a back closet, but it was narrow. Certainly not large enough for...

"If it isn't, then it looks like we might be here for a while." He went to the door and addressed the official. "We haven't opened the tissue samples yet. My assistant has a family. I'd like her to go home before we begin."

Ben had insisted his office be housed in a separate building from the main hospital for just this reason. It was small enough that the whole thing could be sealed off in the event of an airborne epidemic. And just like the microbial test he'd completed for a colleague moments earlier, any results could be sent off via computer.

Safety was his number-one priority. Mandy knew the risks of working for him, but she'd been exposed to nothing, as far as he could tell. Not like when Tracy had rushed headlong into a yellow fever epidemic four years ago that had forced him to call in the military authorities.

The guard in the doorway tapped his foot for a second, as if considering Ben's request. He then turned away and spoke to someone through his walkie-talkie. When he was done, he faced them. "We'll have someone escort her home, but she'll have to remain there until we know what the illness is. As for you two..." he motioned to Ben and Tracy "...once the samples are uncapped you'll have to stay in this building until we determine the risks."

Mandy sent Ben a panicked look. "Are you sure it's safe

for me to leave? My baby..." She shut her eyes. "I need to call my husband."

"Have Sergio take the baby to your mother's house, where she'll be safe. just in case. I'll call you as soon as I know something, okay?"

His assistant nodded and left to make her call.

"I'm sorry." Tracy's face softened. "I thought you'd be alone in the lab. I didn't realize you'd gotten an assistant."

"It's not your fault. She's worried about the risks to her baby." His eyes came up to meet hers, and he couldn't resist the dig. "Just as any woman with children would be."

He mentally kicked himself when the compassion in Tracy's eyes dissolved, and anger took its place.

"I *was* concerned. But it was never enough for you, was it?" Her chest rose as she took a deep breath. "I'm heading back to São João dos Rios as soon as you give me some answers. If I'm going to be quarantined, I'm going to do it where I can make a difference. That doesn't include sitting in a lab, staring at rows of test tubes."

He knew he'd struck a nerve, but it didn't stop an old hurt from creeping up his spine. "Says the woman who came to *my* lab, asking for help," he said quietly.

"I didn't mean it like that."

"Sure you did."

They stared at each other then the corners of her eyes crinkled. She pulled down her mask, letting it dangle around her neck. "Okay, maybe I did...a little. But at least I admitted that I need you. That has to count for something."

It did. But that kind of need was a far cry from what they'd once had together. Those days were long gone, and no matter how hard Ben had tried to hold onto her back then, she'd drifted further and further away, until the gulf between them had been too huge to span.

Bellyaching about the past won't get you anywhere.

Ben shook off the thoughts and set the insulated bag on

an empty metal table. He nodded towards the aluminum glove dispenser hanging on the far wall. "Suit up and don't touch anything in the lab, just in case."

She dug into her handbag instead and pulled out her own box of gloves. "I came prepared."

Of course she had. It was part of who she was. This was a woman who was always on the move—who never took a weekend off. Tracy had thrown herself into her work without restraint…until there had been nothing left for herself. Or for him.

He'd thought she'd stop once the pregnancy tests went from blue to pink. She hadn't. And Ben hadn't been able to face any child of his going through what he had as a kid.

Gritting his teeth in frustration, he glanced around the lab, eyeing the centrifuges and other equipment. They'd have to work in the tiny glassed-off cubicle in the corner that he'd set up for occasions like this.

Keeping his day-to-day work space absolutely separate from Tracy's samples was not only smart, it was non-negotiable. If they weren't careful, the government could end up quarantining his whole lab, meaning years of work would be tossed into the incinerator. He tensed. Although if their findings turned up a microbe that was airborne, he'd willingly burn everything himself. He wouldn't risk setting loose an epidemic.

Not even for Tracy. She should know that by now.

"I have a clean room set up over there. Once we get things squared away with Mandy, we can start."

Tracy peered towards the door where the phone conversation between his assistant and her husband was growing more heated by the second. "I was really careful about keeping everything as sterile as I could. I don't think she's been exposed to anything."

"I'm sure it'll be fine. I'm going to take your bagged

samples into the other area. Can you wipe down the table where they were with disinfectant?"

As soon as Ben picked up the insulated bag, the guard appeared, his hand resting on the butt of his gun. "Where are you going with that?"

Ben motioned towards the clean room. "The samples can't infect anyone else if they're kept enclosed. You can see everything we do from the reception doorway. It'll be safer if you keep your distance once we've started testing, though."

The guard backed up a couple of paces. "How long will it take? I have no wish to stay here any longer than I have to."

"I have no idea. It depends on what we're dealing with."

Putting the bag in the cubicle, he gathered the equipment he'd need and arranged it on the set of metal shelves perched above a stainless-steel table. He blew out a breath. The eight-by-eight-foot area was going to be cramped once he and Tracy were both inside.

An air handler filtered any particles floating in and out of the clean room, but there was no safe way to pump air-conditioning into the space. They'd have to rely on the wheezy window unit in the main lab and hope it kept them from baking. He could offer to send Tracy on her way before he got the results—but he was pretty sure he knew how that suggestion would be met, despite her waspish words earlier.

You couldn't coax—or force—Tracy to do anything she didn't want to do. He knew that from experience.

Mandy appeared in the doorway to the reception area just as Ben turned on the air filter and closed the door on the samples.

"It's all arranged. Sergio called my mom and asked if she'd care for the baby overnight. He's not happy about staying home from work, but he doesn't want me to stay here either."

"I don't blame him. But look on the bright side. At least you can go home." He smiled. "Tell Sergio he should count his lucky stars I haven't stolen you away from him."

Mandy laughed. "You've already told him that yourself. Many times."

Tracy spun away from them and stalked over to the metal table she'd previously sanitized and began scrubbing it all over again. She kept her head down, not looking at either of them.

"Is the guard going to take you home?" He forced the words to remain cheerful.

"They're sending another policeman. He should be here soon."

"Good." He had Mandy go back and wait in the reception area, so there'd be no question of her being anywhere near those samples. Returning to the sealed cubicle, he slid the insulated bag into a small refrigerator he kept for just this purpose. The air was already growing close inside the room, but he'd worked under worse conditions many times before. Both he and Tracy had.

He could still picture one such occasion—their very first meeting—Tracy had stepped off the *Projeto Vida* medical boat and stalked into the village he had been surveying, demanding to know what he was doing about the malaria outbreak twenty miles downriver. He'd been exhausted, and she'd looked like a gorgeous avenging angel, silky black hair flowing behind her in the breeze, ready to slay him if he said one wrong word.

They'd barely lasted two days before they'd fallen into bed together.

Something he'd rather not remember at the moment. Especially as he was trying to avoid any and all physical contact with her.

She might be immune, but he wasn't. Not judging from the way his heart had taken off at a sprint when he'd seen her standing in that doorway.

Tracy dumped her paper towel into the hazardous waste receptacle and crossed over to him. "I just want to say thank you for agreeing to help. You could have told me to get lost." She gave a hard laugh. "I wouldn't have blamed you if you had."

"I'm not always an ogre, you know."

Her teeth caught the right corner of her bottom lip in a way that made his chest tighten. "I know. And I'm sorry for dragging you into this, but I didn't know where else to go. The military didn't want me to take the samples out of São João dos Rios. They only agreed to let me come here because you've worked with them before…and even then they made me bring a guard. I honestly didn't think anyone else would be affected other than us."

"It's not your fault, Trace." He started to reach out to touch her cheek, but checked himself. "The government is probably right to keep this as contained as possible. If I thought there was any chance of contamination, I'd be the first one to say Mandy needs to stay here at the lab with us."

He smiled. "If I know you, though, not one microbe survived on that bag before you carried it out of that town."

"I hope not. There are still several ill people waiting on us for answers. I left a colleague behind to make sure the military didn't do anything rash, but he's not a doctor, and I don't want to risk his health either." She blew out a breath. "Those people need help. But there's nothing I can do until I know what we're dealing with."

And then she'd be on her way to the next available crisis. Just like she always was.

His smile faded. "Let's get to work, then."

The guard stuck his head into the room. "They're sending someone for your friend. They'll keep her at home until the danger has passed."

Ben nodded. "I understand. Thank you."

When he went to the doorway to say goodbye to Mandy, she kissed his cheek, her arms circling his neck and hugging him close. When she finally let go, her eyes shimmered with unshed tears. "I'm so grateful. I can't imagine not being able to tuck my Jenny into bed tonight, but at least I'll be closer to her than I would be if I stayed here."

His heart clenched. Here was a woman whose baby meant the world to her—who didn't need to jet off to distant places to find fulfillment. Unlike his parents.

Unlike Tracy.

"We'll work as quickly as we can. Once things are clear, make sure you give her a kiss and a hug from her uncle Ben."

"I will." She wiped a spot of lipstick from his cheek with her thumb. "Be careful, okay? I've just gotten used to your crazy ways. I don't want to break someone else in."

Ben laughed and took off one of his latex gloves, laying his hand on her shoulder. "You're not getting rid of me any time soon, so go and enjoy your mini-vacation. You'll be back to the same old grind before you know it."

Mandy's escort arrived, and as soon as she exited the building, he turned back to find Tracy observing him with a puzzled frown.

"What?" he asked.

She shrugged. "Nothing. I'm just surprised you haven't found a woman who'd be thrilled to stick close to the house and give you all those kids you said you wanted."

"That would be impossible, given the circumstances."

"Oh?" Her brows arched. "And why is that?"

He laughed, the sound harsh in the quiet room. "Do you really have to ask?"

"I just did."

Grabbing her left hand, he held it up, forcing her eyes to the outline of the plain gold band visible beneath her latex glove. "For the same reason you're wearing this." He stared into her face. "Have you forgotten, *Mrs. Almeida*? You may not go by your married name any more, but in the eyes of the law…we're still husband and wife."

CHAPTER TWO

SHE'D FORGOTTEN NOTHING.

And she'd tried to see about getting a divorce, but being overseas made everything a hundred times more complicated. Both of the Brazilian lawyers she'd contacted had said that as an American citizen, she should return to the States and start the proceedings there, as she and Ben had been married in New York. But asking him to accompany her had been out of the question. Even if he'd been willing, she wasn't. She hadn't wanted to be anywhere near him, too raw from everything that had transpired in the month before she'd left *Teresina*—and him—for ever.

Staying married probably hadn't been the wisest move on her part but she'd thrown herself into her work afterwards, far too busy with *Projeto Vida*, her aid organization's floating clinic, to set the ugly wheels in motion. Besides, a wedding ring tended to scare away any man who ventured too close. Not that there'd been many. Her *caution-do-not-touch* vibes must be coming through loud and clear. She'd never get married again—to anyone—so keeping her wedding ring and her license made keeping that promise a whole lot easier.

Too bad she hadn't remembered to take the ring off before asking Ben for help.

She realized he was still waiting for a response so she lifted her chin, praying he wouldn't notice the slight tremble. "We're not married any more. Not by any stretch of the imagination. You made sure of that."

"Right." Ben turned away and gathered a few more pieces of equipment.

Her thumb instinctively rubbed back and forth across the ring, a gesture she'd found oddly comforting during some of the tougher periods of her life—like now.

Strange how most of those times had found her wearing surgical gloves.

Studying Ben as he worked, Tracy was surprised by the slight dusting of grey in his thick brown hair. She gave herself a mental shake. The man was thirty-eight, and she hadn't set eyes on him in four years. Change was inevitable. What hadn't changed, however, were the electric blue eyes, compliments of his American mother, or how they provided the perfect counterpoint for tanned skin, high cheekbones and a straight, autocratic nose—all legacies from his Brazilian father. Neither had he lost any of that intense focus she'd once found so intimidating.

And irresistible.

Snap out of it, Tracy.

She donned the scrubs, booties and surgical gear Ben had left out for her and moved into the glassed-in cubicle where he was busy setting up.

"Close the door, please, so I can seal it off."

"Seal it off?" Swallowing hard, she hesitated then did as he asked.

"Just with this." He held up a roll of clear packing tape. "Is your claustrophobia going to be a problem?"

She hoped not, but feeling trapped had always set off a rolling sense of panic that could quickly snowball if she wasn't careful. It didn't matter whether the confinement was physical or emotional, the fear was the same. Glancing through the door to the reception area, she noted the exit to the outside world was plainly visible even from where she stood. "As long as I know there's a door right through there, I should be fine. The room being made of glass helps."

"Good."

Ben taped the edges of the door, before removing the insulated bag from the fridge and examining the labels on each tube inside. Selecting two of them, he put the rest back in cold storage.

"What do you want me to do?" Tracy asked.

"Set up some slides. We're going to work our way from simple to complex."

He turned one of the tubes to the side and read her label out loud. "Daniel, male, twelve years." He paused. "Living?"

"Yes." Her heart twisted when she thought of the preteen boy staring at her with terrified eyes. But at least he was alive. As was his younger sister Cleo. Their mother, however, hadn't been so lucky. Hers had been one of the first bodies they'd found in the village. "Febrile. No skin lesions visible."

"Signs of pneumonia?"

"Not yet, which is why this seemed so strange. Most of the dead had complained to relatives of coughs along with fever and malaise."

"Liver enlargement in the dead?"

She swallowed. "No autopsies, remember? The military destroyed everything." Her voice cracked.

Ben's gloved hand covered hers, and even through the layers of latex the familiar warmth of his touch comforted her in a way no one else ever could. "Why don't you get those slides ready, while I set up the centrifuge?"

Glad to have something to take her mind off the horrific scene she and Pedro had stumbled on in São João dos Rios, she pulled several clean slides from the box and spread them across the table. Then, carefully taking the cotton swab from Ben's outstretched hand, she smeared a thin layer of material on the smooth glass surface. "What are you looking for?"

"Anything. Everything." The tense muscle in his jaw made her wonder if he already had a theory. "You'll need to heat-set the slides as you smear them."

He lit a small burner and showed her how to pass the slide across the flame to dry it and affix the specimen to the glass.

The sound of a throat clearing in the outer doorway made them both look up. Their guard cupped his hands over his mouth and said in a loud voice, "Your assistant has arrived safely at her home."

Ben flashed a thumbs-up sign. "Thanks for letting me know."

Tracy's fingers tensed on the slide at the mention of Ben's assistant, which was ridiculous. Yes, the woman had kissed him, but Brazilians kissed everyone—it was a kind of unspoken rule in these parts. Besides, the woman had a family. A new baby.

Her throat tightened, a sense of loss sweeping over her. Ben had wanted children so badly. So had she. When she'd fallen pregnant, they'd both been elated. Until she'd had a devastating piece of news that had set her back on her heels. She'd thrown herself into her work, angering Ben, even as she'd tried to figure out a way to tell him.

That had all changed when he'd sent the military in to force her out of a stricken village during a yellow fever outbreak. She knew he'd been trying to protect her and the baby—not from the disease itself, as she'd already been vaccinated the previous year, but from anything that had taken her out of his sight. She hadn't need protecting, though. She'd needed to work. It had been her lifeline in a time of turmoil and confusion, and his interference had damaged her trust. She'd miscarried a week later, and the

rift that had opened between them during their disagree-
ment over the military had grown deeper, with accusations
flying fast and furious on both sides.

In the end she'd opted to keep her secret to herself. Telling him would have changed nothing, not when she'd already decided to leave.

Work was still her number-one priority. Still her lifeline. And she needed to get her mind back on what she
was doing.

Tracy took the long cotton swab and dipped it into another of her sample jars, laying a thin coating of the material on a second glass slide, heat-setting it, like she'd done
with the first. "Do you need me to apply a stain?"

"Let's see what we've got on these first."

"There were pigs in a corral at one of the victims'
homes. Could it be leptospirosis?"

"Possibly." He switched on the microscope's light. "If
I can't find anything on the slides, we'll need to do some
cultures. Lepto will show up there."

He didn't say it, but they both knew cultures would take
several days, if not longer, to grow.

Tracy sent a nervous glance towards the reception area,
where the guard lounged in a white plastic chair in full
view. He twirled what looked like a toothpick between
his thumb and forefinger. For the moment his attention
wasn't focused on them. And he was far enough away
that he shouldn't be able to hear soft voices through the
glass partition.

"That could be a problem."

Ben turned toward her, watchful eyes moving over her
face. "How so?"

"I told the military police you'd have an answer for
them today."

"You did *what*?" His hand clenched on the edge of the
table. "Of all the irresponsible—"

"I know, I know. I didn't have a choice. It was either that or leave São João dos Rios empty-handed."

He closed his eyes for a few seconds before looking at her again. "You're still hauling around that savior complex, aren't you, Tracy? Don't you get tired of being the one who swoops in to save the day?"

"I thought that was *your* role. Taking charge even when it's not your decision to make." She tossed her head. "Maybe if you'd stopped thinking about yourself for once…" As soon as the ugly words spurted out she gritted her teeth, staunching the flow. "I'm sorry. That was uncalled for."

"Yes. It was." He took the slide from her and set it down with an audible *crack*.

The guard was on his feet in an instant, his casual manner gone. *"O que foi?"*

Ben held up the slide. "Sorry. Just dropped it." Although he said the words loudly enough for the guard to hear them, he kept his tone calm and even. Even so, the tension in his white-knuckled grip was unmistakable.

The guard rolled his eyes, his face relaxing. "I'm going to the cafeteria. Do you want something?"

How exactly did the man expect to get the food past the sealed doorway? Besides, she wouldn't be able to eat if her life depended on it. "I'm good. Thanks."

"Same here," said Ben.

The guard shrugged and then checked the front door. He palmed the old-fashioned key he found in the lock before reinserting it again, this time on the outside of the door.

He meant to lock them in!

"No, wait!" Tracy stood, not exactly sure how she could stop him.

"Sorry, but I have my orders. Neither of you leaves until those samples are destroyed."

She started to argue further, but Ben touched her shoulder. "Don't," he said in a low voice.

Holding her tongue, she watched helplessly as the door swung shut, a menacing snick of the lock telling her the guard had indeed imprisoned them inside the room. A familiar sting of panic went up her spine. "What if he doesn't come back? What if we're trapped?"

Stripping off one of his gloves, he reached into his pocket. "I have a spare. I know you don't like being confined."

Sagging in relief, she managed a shaky laugh. "You learned that the hard way, didn't you?"

The vivid image of Ben playfully pinning her hands above her head while they'd tussled on the bed sprang to her mind. The love play had been fun. At first. Then a wave of terror had washed over her unexpectedly, and though she'd known her panic had been illogical, she'd begun to struggle in earnest.

A frightened plea had caught in her throat, and as hard as she'd tried to say something, her voice had seemed as frozen as her senses. Ben had only realized she was no longer playing when she succeeded in freeing one of her hands and raked her nails down his face. He'd reeled backwards, while she'd lain there, her chest heaving, tears of relief spilling from her eyes. Understanding had dawned on his face and he'd gathered her into his arms, murmuring how sorry he was. From that moment forward he'd been careful to avoid anything that might make her feel trapped.

A little too careful.

His lovemaking had become less intense and more controlled. Only it had been a different kind of control than what they'd previously enjoyed, when Ben's take-charge demeanor in the bedroom had been a huge turn-on. That had all changed. Tracy had mourned the loss of passion, even as she'd appreciated his reasons for keeping a little more space between them. Her inability to explain where the line between confinement and intimacy lay had driven the first wedge between them.

That wedge had widened later, when he'd tried to limit her movements during her pregnancy, giving rise to the same sensation of being suffocated. She'd clawed at him just as hard then, the marks invisible but causing just as much damage to their marriage.

The Ben of the present fingered the side of his face and gave her a smile. "No permanent damage done."

Yeah, there had been. And it seemed that one patch of bad luck had spiraled into another.

"I always felt terrible about that," she said.

"I should have realized you were scared."

"You couldn't have known."

Even her father hadn't realized their play sessions could change without warning. There'd always been laughter, but the sound of hers had often turned shrill with overtones of panic. A gentle soul, her father would have never hurt her in a million years. It didn't help that her older sister had been a tough-as-nails tomboy who'd feared nothing and had given as good as she'd got. Then Tracy had come along—always fearful, always more cautious. Her father had never quite known what to do with her.

She was still fearful. Still flinched away from situations that made her feel trapped and out of control.

And now her mom and her sister were both gone. Her mom, the victim of a menacing villain who'd stalked its prey relentlessly—turning the delicate strands of a person's DNA into the enemy. Passed from mother to daughter. Tracy had been running from its specter ever since.

Ben donned a fresh glove and picked up the slide he'd smacked against the table, checking it for cracks. Without glancing up at her, he said, "You look tired. I put the folding cot in the corner in case we needed to sleep in shifts. If I know you, you didn't get much rest last night."

"I'm okay." He was right. She was exhausted, but no way would she let him know how easily he could still read her. Or how the touch of concern in his voice made her heart skip a beat. "It's just warm in here."

"I know. The air-conditioner in the lab is ancient, and the filter doesn't let much of it through, anyway."

Even as he said it, a tiny trickle of sweat coursed down her back. "It's fine."

He pushed the slide beneath the viewer of the microscope and focused on the smear. "How old are the samples?"

"Just a couple of hours."

He swore softly as he continued to peer through the lens, evidently seeing something he didn't like. He took the second slide and repeated the process, his right hand shifting a knob on the side of the instrument repeatedly. Sitting up, he dabbed at perspiration that had gathered around his eye with the sleeve of his lab coat then leaned back in for another look.

"What is it?" She felt her own blood rushing through her ears as she awaited the verdict.

It didn't take long. He lifted his head and fastened his eyes on hers. "If I'm not mistaken, it's pneumonic plague, Tracy." Shifting his attention to the test tube in her hand, he continued, "And if you're the one who took these samples, you've already been exposed."

CHAPTER THREE

TRACY SAGGED AND swallowed hard, trying to process what he'd said through her own fear. "Are you sure?"

"Here." He moved aside so she could look at the slide.

Putting her eye to the viewfinder, she squinted into the machine. "What am I looking for?"

"See the little dots grouped into chains?"

"Yes." There were several of them.

"That's what we're dealing with. I want to look at another sample and do a culture, just in case, but I'm sure. It's *Yersinia pestis*, the same bacterium that causes bubonic plague. I recognize the shape." He rolled his shoulders as if relieving an ache. "Bubonic plague normally spreads from infected rats through the bite of a flea, but if the bacteria migrate to a person's lungs, it becomes even more deadly, spreading rapidly from person to person by way of a cough or bodily fluids. When that happens, the disease no longer needs a flea. We'll want to put you on a strong dose of streptomycin immediately."

"What about you?"

"I'll start on them as well, but just as a precaution." Ben dripped a staining solution on another slide. "Most of the people who work in the lab are vaccinated against the plague, including Mandy. But I assume you haven't been."

"No, which means neither has… Oh, God." She rested her head against Ben's shoulder for a second as a wave of nausea rolled over her. "That town. I have to get back there. They've all been exposed. So has Pedro."

"Pedro?"

"*My* assistant."

Just as he pushed the slide back under the microscope, the lock to the outer door clicked open before Tracy had a chance to figure out how to proceed.

The guard pushed his way inside, glancing from one to the other, his eyes narrowing in on her face. She sat up straighter.

"Problema?" he asked.

Instead of lunch, he only held a coffee cup in his hand.

A tug on the back of her shirt sent a warning Tracy read loud and clear, *Don't tell him anything until I've taken another look.* The gesture surprised her, as he'd always been buddy-buddy with the military, at least from what she'd seen over the course of their marriage.

Still holding one of the slides, he casually laid it on the table. "We need to run a few more tests before we know anything for sure."

"No need. Our doctors have isolated the infection and will take the appropriate containment measures."

Containment? What exactly did that mean?

Her brows lifted in challenge. "What is the illness, then?" Maybe he was bluffing.

"I'm not at liberty to say. But my commander would like to speak with Dr. Almeida over the phone." He gave Tracy a pointed stare. "Alone."

A shiver went over her. Alone. Why?

What if the government doctors had come to a different conclusion than Ben had? What if they were assuming it was something other than the plague? People could still die…still pass it on to neighboring towns. And São João dos Rios was poor. How many people would lose loved ones due to lack of information?

Just like she had. She knew the pain of that firsthand.

She'd lost her mother. Her grandmother. Her sister—although Vickie's illness hadn't been related to a genetic defect. The most devastating loss of all, however, had been her unborn child. Ben's baby.

All had died far too young. And Tracy had decided she wasn't going to waste a second of her time on earth waiting around for what-ifs. Movement, in her eyes, equaled life. So she'd lived that life with a ferocity that others couldn't begin to understand.

Including Ben.

Genetic code might not be written in stone, but its deadly possibility loomed in front of her, as did a decision she might someday choose to make. But until then she was determined to make a difference in the lives of those around her.

Or maybe you're simply running away.

Like she had with Ben? No, their break-up had been for entirely different reasons.

Had it?

She pushed the voice in her head aside. "Why does he want to talk to Dr. Almeida alone?"

"That's not for me to say." The guard nodded towards the bag. "Those samples must be destroyed."

"We'll take care of it." Her husband's voice was calm. Soothing. Just as Zen-like as ever. Just as she imagined it would have been had she told him about the life-changing decision she was wrestling with.

And his icy unflappability drove her just as crazy now as it had during their last fight.

How could he take everything in his stride?

Because it was part of who he was. He'd grown up in Brazil…was more Brazilian than American in a lot of ways.

As Ben stripped the tape from around the door and

sanitized his hands before stepping into the hallway with the guard, Tracy sighed. She never knew what he was thinking. Even during their marriage he'd been tight-lipped about a lot of things. But as aloof as he'd been at times, she'd sensed something in him yearning for what he hadn't had when growing up: the closeness of a family.

It still hurt that she hadn't been able to give that to him. That even as she was driven to work harder and harder by the loss of her baby and by whatever time bomb might be ticking inside her, she was gradually becoming the very thing he despised in his parents.

Her sister had died never knowing whether or not she carried the defective gene. It hadn't been cancer that had claimed Vickie's life but dengue fever—a disease that was endemic in Brazil. She'd been pregnant at the time of her death. Her husband had been devastated at losing both of them. As had she. But at least Vickie had been spared the agonizing uncertainty over whether or not she'd passed a cancer gene down to her child.

As much as Tracy had feared doing just that during her pregnancy, she'd never in her weakest moments wished harm to come to her unborn child. And yet she'd lost the baby anyway, as if even the fates knew what a bad idea it was for her to reproduce.

Her vision suddenly went blurry, and she blinked in an effort to clear her head from those painful thoughts. As she did, she realized Ben and the guard had come back into the room and were now staring at her.

"What?" she asked, mentally daring him to say anything about her moist eyes.

Ben's gaze sharpened, but he said nothing. "I need to leave for São João dos Rios. Do you want me to drop you off at the airport on my way out of town?"

"Excuse me?"

Why would she need to go to the airport? Unless…

No way!

Her hands went to her hips. "I'm going with you."

Both Ben and the guard spoke at once, their voices jumbled. She caught the gist of it, however. Evidently Ben had been invited to go but she hadn't been.

Outrage crowded her chest. "I'm the one who took the samples. I've already been out there."

"And exposed yourself to the plague in the process."

"Exactly." Her hands dropped back to her sides, palms out. "I've already been exposed. And I'm a doctor, Ben. I've spent my life fighting outbreaks like this one. I should be there."

His voice cooled. "It's not up to me this time."

"*This* time. Unlike the time you sent your goons into that village with orders to send me packing?" She almost spit the words at him. "My assistant is still in São João dos Rios. I am not leaving him out there alone."

Stepping around Ben, she focused on the guard. "I'd like to speak with your superior."

The man blinked several times, as if he couldn't believe she was daring to defy whatever orders he'd received. "I'm afraid that's not possible—"

Ben's fingers went around her upper arm and squeezed. "Let me talk to her for a minute."

Practically dragging her to the other side of the room, his stony gaze fastened on her face. "What are you doing?"

"I already told you. I'm doing my job."

"The military wants to handle this their way. They'll go in and treat those who aren't too far gone and make sure this doesn't spread beyond São João dos Rios."

"Those who aren't too far gone? My God, stop and listen to yourself for a minute. We're talking about human beings—about children like Daniel and Cleo, who are now orphans. They deserve someone there who will fight for them."

"You think I don't care about those children? I was the one who wanted you to slow down during your pregnancy, to…" He paused for several long seconds then lowered his voice. "I care just as much about those villagers as you do."

His surgeon's scalpel cut deep. She could guess what he'd been about to say before he'd checked himself. He still thought her actions had cost the life of their child. And the worst thing was that she couldn't say with any certainty that he was wrong. She'd worked herself harder than ever after she'd had the results back from the genetic testing—struggling to beat back the familiar sensation of being trapped. But that wasn't something she wanted to get into right now.

"Let me go with you." She twisted out of his grasp so she could turn and face him. "Please. You have pull with these guys, I know you do. Call the commander back, whoever he is, and tell him you need me."

He dragged a hand through his hair then shook his head. "I'm asking you to walk away, Tracy. Just this once. You don't know how bad things might get before it's over."

"I do know. That's why I need to be there. Those two kids have already lost their mother. I want to help make sure they don't lose their lives as well."

She was not going to let some government bureaucrat—or even Ben—decide they were a lost cause. "I'll take antibiotics while I'm there. I'll do whatever the government people tell me to do. Besides, like I said before, my assistant is still in the middle of it."

She couldn't explain to him that she really did need to be there. This was part of what being alive meant—fighting battles for others that she might not be able to fight for herself. She took a deep breath. "Please, don't make me beg."

A brief flicker of something went across his face then was gone. "Listen, I know—" Before he could finish the guard appeared in front of them, tapping his hat against his thigh, clearly impatient to be gone. "We need to leave."

Tracy kept her pleading gaze focused on Ben. *He had to let her go. He just had to.*

Ben swore and then broke eye contact. "Call General Gutierrez and tell him we're on our way. Both of us."

The man didn't bat an eyelid. "I'll let him know."

Exactly how much influence did Ben have with these officials? She knew his salary came from the government, but to say something like that and expect it to be accepted without question…

She swallowed. "Thank you."

Jaw tight, Ben ignored her and addressed the guard again. "We'll follow you out to the village once I've destroyed the samples. We need to use my four-wheel drive to haul some equipment."

The guard swept his hat onto his head before relaying the message to his superiors. When he finished the call, he said, "My commander will have someone meet you at the town square and direct you to the triage area they've set up. But you must hurry."

Ben nodded. "Tell them we'll be there within three hours."

"Vai com Deus."

The common "Go with God" farewell had an ominous ring to it—as if the man had crossed himself in an attempt to ward off evil. And pneumonic plague was all that and more. Its cousin had killed off large swaths of the world's population in the past.

Despite her misgivings about working with Ben again, a couple of muscles in her stomach relaxed. At least she wouldn't have to fight this particular battle on her own.

Ben would be there with her.

And if he found out the truth about the genetic testing she'd had done before their separation?

Then she would deal with it. Just as she'd dealt with the loss of her baby and her own uncertain prognosis.

Alone.

As they hurried to finish loading his vehicle, a streak of lightning darted across the sky, pausing to lick the trunk of a nearby tree before sliding back into the clouds. The smell of singed wood reached Ben a few seconds later, followed by an ominous rumble that made the ground tremble.

Tracy, who stood beside him, shuddered. "Only in *Teresina*."

He smiled. "Remember the city's nickname? *Chapada do corisco:* flash-lightning flatlands. If ever lightning was going to strike twice in the same spot, it would be here." He shut the back of the grey four-wheel-drive vehicle. "I'd rather not put that theory to the test, though, so, if you're ready to go, hop in."

She climbed into the SUV and buckled in, staring in the direction the jagged flash had come from. "That poor tree looks like it's lightning's favorite prom date, judging from the color."

Scarred from multiple strikes over the years, it stubbornly clung to life, clusters of green leaves scattered along its massive branches. Ben had no idea how it had survived so many direct hits.

Their marriage certainly hadn't been as lucky.

He got behind the wheel and started the car. "It'll eventually have to come down."

"Through no fault of its own," she murmured. "It's sad."

Was she thinking of what had happened between them? It had taken every ounce of strength he'd had after she'd left, but he'd forced himself to keep living. In reality, though, she had been gone long before she'd actually moved out of the house. He'd accepted it and moved forward.

Right.

That's why he was on his way to São João dos Rios right now, with Tracy in tow. He should have just shut her down and said no. General Gutierrez would have backed him in his decision. So why hadn't he?

"You sure you want to do this? The airport is on our way. We could still have you on a flight to São Paulo in a jiffy."

She jerked in her seat, gripping the webbing of the seat belt before shifting to look at him. "I can't just turn my back on the town. That's not how I operate."

Really? It had seemed all too easy for her to turn her back on him. But saying so wouldn't help anyone.

They reached the entrance to the highway, and Ben sighed when he saw metal barricades stretched across its width.

The four-lane road—long under construction—was still not finished.

He coasted down a steep incline to reach the so-called official detour, which consisted of a narrow dirt track running parallel to the road. It looked more like a gully from water run-off than an actual street. As far as the eye could see, where the highway should have been there was now a long stretch of hard-packed orange clay that was impassable. At the moment trucks seemed to be the only vehicles braving the washboard tract Ben and Tracy were forced to use. Then again, there was no other option. Most things, including food, were moved from city to city via semi-tractor-trailers. And with the current conditions of the highway it was no wonder things were so expensive in northeastern Brazil.

"How long have they been working on this?" Tracy asked.

"Do you really need to ask?"

"No. But it *was* paved the last time I was here."

They'd spent most of their marriage in *Teresina*, the capital of the state of *Piaui*. He'd rearranged his job so he could stay in one place. Ben thought Tracy had been willing to do the same. How wrong he'd been.

She *had* come off the medical boat and put someone else in her place, but that was about the only concession she'd made to their marriage. By the time he'd realized she was never going to slow down, he'd lost more than just his wife.

"Yes, it was paved, after a fashion." He grimaced. "I think the shoulder we're on is in better shape than the highway was back then."

Ben slowed to navigate a particularly bad stretch where torrential rains had worn a deep channel into the dirt. "Well, some parts of it, anyway."

"My car would never survive the trip."

He smiled. "Are you still driving that little tin can?"

"Rhonda gets great gas mileage."

His gut twisted. He could still remember the laughter they'd shared over Tracy's insistence on keeping her ragamuffin car when they'd got married, despite the hazardous stretches of road in Teresina. To his surprise, the little vehicle had been sturdier than it had appeared, bumping along the worst of the cobblestone streets with little more than an occasional hiccup. Like the bumper she'd lost on a visit to one of the neighboring *aldéias*. She'd come back with the thing strapped to the roof. He smiled. When he'd suggested it was time to trade the vehicle in, she'd refused, patting the bonnet and saying the car had seen her through some tough spots.

His smile faded. Funny how her loyalty to her car hadn't been mirrored in her marriage.

He cast around for a different subject, but Tracy got there first.

"How's Marcelo doing?"

Ben's brother was the new chief of neurosurgery over

at Teresina's main hospital. "He's fine. Still as opinion-
ated as ever."

She smiled. "Translated to mean he's still single."

"Always will be, if he has his way." He glanced over at
her. "What about you? How's *Projeto Vida* going?" The
medical-aid ship that had brought them together was still
Tracy's pet project.

"Wonderfully. Matt is back on the team and has a baby
girl now."

Tracy's sister had died years ago, leaving her husband,
Matt, heartbroken. "He remarried?"

"Yep. Two years ago." She paused. "Stevie…Stephani,
actually, is great. She loves the job and fits right into the
team."

"I'm glad. Matt seemed like a nice guy." Ben had met
him on several occasions when they'd traveled to *Coari* to
deliver supplies or check on the medical boat.

"He is. It's good to see him happy again."

Which was more than he could say about Tracy. Maybe
it was the stress of what she'd been dealing with in São
João dos Rios, but the dark circles under her green eyes
worried him. He glanced to the side for a quick peek. The
rest of her looked exactly as he remembered, though. Long,
silky black hair that hung just below her shoulders. The
soft fringe of bangs that fluttered whenever the flow from
the air-conditioning vent caught the strands. Lean, tanned
legs encased in khaki shorts.

And as much as he wished otherwise, being near her
again made him long for family and normalcy all over
again. He'd always thought she would bring stability to
his life, help to counteract his tumultuous upbringing. His
parents had drifted here and there, always searching for
a new adventure while leaving their two young sons in
the care of their housekeeper. In many ways, Ben had felt
closer to Rosa than to his own mother, so much so that he'd

kept her on at his house long after his parents had moved to the States on a permanent basis.

He'd thought life with Tracy would be different. That their children would have the close-knit family he'd always longed for as a kid. But Tracy, once the first blush of their marriage had faded, had started traveling again, always finding some new medical crisis to deal with, whether with *Projeto Vida* or somewhere else.

He could understand being married to your career—after all, he was pretty attached to his—but he'd learned to do it from one central location. Surely Tracy could have done the same.

Instead, with every month that had passed, the same feelings of abandonment he'd had as a kid had taken root and grown, as had his resentment. And once she'd fallen pregnant, she'd seemed more obsessed about work than ever, spending longer and longer periods away from home.

When he'd learned she was dealing with a yellow fever outbreak in one of the villages he'd finally snapped and called his old friend General Gutierrez—despite the fact that he knew Tracy been vaccinated against the disease. His ploy had worked. Tracy had come home. But their marriage had been over, even before she'd lost the baby.

So why hadn't he just settled down with someone else, like Tracy had suggested a few hours earlier? Marriage wasn't exactly a requirement these days. And why hadn't Tracy finally asked for a divorce and been done with it?

Questions he was better off not asking.

"What's the time frame for pneumonic plague?"

Her question jolted him back to the present. "From exposure to presentation of symptoms? Two days, on average. Although death can take anywhere from thirty-six hours after exposure to a week or more. It depends on whether or not other organ systems besides the lungs have been compromised."

"Oh, no."

"Speaking of which, I've brought packets of antibiotics in that black gym bag I threw in the back. Go ahead and dig through it and take a dose before we get there."

Tracy unhooked her seat belt and twisted until she could reach the backseat. She then pulled out one of the boxes of medicine and popped a pill from the protective foil. She downed it with a swig from her water bottle then shoved a couple of strands of hair back from her temple. "You have no idea how glad I am that you were able figure it out so quickly."

"I think I do." Surely she realized he was just as relieved as she was. "Not everyone has the equipment we do."

"Or the backing of the military."

He ignored the bitterness that colored her words. "Part of the reality of living in a developing country. We'll catch up with the rest of the world, eventually. Marcelo's hospital is a great example of that. It's completely funded by sources outside the government."

"So is *Projeto Vida*." She paused when they hit another rough patch of road, her hand scrabbling for the grip attached to the ceiling. "Speaking of funding, we'll need to check with the nearest pharmacist to make sure they have enough antibiotics on hand. I'll pay for more, if need be."

"I was already planning to help with the costs." He glanced over and their eyes caught for a second. When he turned his attention back to the road, her fingers slid over the hand he had resting on the emergency brake before retreating.

"Thank you, Ben," she said. "For letting me come. And for caring about what happens to those people."

He swallowed, her words and the warmth of her fingers

penetrating the icy wall he'd built up over the last four years.

It wasn't exactly the thing that peace treaties were made of, but he got the feeling that Tracy had just initiated talks.

And had thrown the ball squarely into his court.

CHAPTER FOUR

MILITARY VEHICLES BLOCKED the road to São João dos Rios—uniformed personnel, guns at the ready, stood beside the vehicles.

"They're not taking any chances," Ben muttered as he slowed the car on the dirt track.

"In this case, caution is probably a good thing." As much as Tracy worried about the presence of the Brazilian army, she also knew the country's military had helped ease Brazil's transition from a Portuguese colony to an independent nation. Not a drop of blood had been shed on either side. The two countries were still on good terms, in fact.

There was no reason to fear their presence. Not really. At least, that's what she told herself.

Ben powered down his window and flashed his residence card, identifying both of them. "General Gutierrez is expecting us."

The soldier checked a handwritten list on his clipboard and nodded. "You've been told what you're dealing with?"

No. They'd been told nothing other than Ben being asked to come, but Tracy wasn't sure how much this particular soldier knew. She didn't want to start a mass panic.

Ben nodded. "We're aware. We brought masks and equipment."

She didn't contradict him or try to add to his words. She knew he'd done quite a bit of work for the military and he'd probably identified many other pathogens for them in the past. They had also taken the time to track her down and challenge her work four years ago, when Ben had asked them to, something that still had the power to make her hackles rise.

The soldier nodded. "I'll need to search your vehicle. General Gutierrez said there were to be no exceptions. So if you'll both step out, please."

Ben glanced her way, before putting the car in neutral—leaving the engine running and nodding at her to get out. He handed her a mask and donned one himself as he climbed from the vehicle.

The soldier looked in the backseat. He then gave the dizzying array of equipment they were carrying a cursory glance but didn't open any of the boxes. He seemed to be looking for stowaways more than anything, which seemed crazy. Who would want to sneak into a plague-infested area? Then again, she'd heard of crazier things, and nobody wanted this disease to get out of the village and into one of the bigger cities. *Teresina* wasn't all that far away, when you thought about it.

Ben came to stand next to her, and she noticed he was careful not to touch her. She swallowed. Not that she wanted him to. She'd had no idea they'd be thrown together in a situation like the one they were currently facing. But despite the pain that seeing him again brought, she couldn't have asked for a better, or more qualified, work partner.

She heard her name being called and turned towards the sound. Pedro hurried toward them, only to be stopped by another soldier about fifty yards before he reached them. The man's point came across loud and clear. Once she and Ben crossed this particular line, there'd be no going back until it was all over. Who knew how long that could be?

"Ben, are you sure you want to do this? You can drop

me off and go back to Teresina. There's no reason to risk yourself and all your work."

A muscle spasmed in his jaw, his eyes on Pedro. "*My* name was the one on the dance card, remember?" He shoved his hands in his pockets. "Besides, this is part of my job. It's why I work at the institute."

"Yes, well…" She didn't know how to finish the statement, since her reasons for wanting him to go back to the safe confines of his office was nothing more than a bid to keep her distance. She'd used his invitation as a way to regain access to the town, but she was also smart enough to know they might need his expertise before this was all over. So she held her tongue.

She glanced back at the soldier, who was currently peering beneath the car at its chassis.

Really? The guy had been watching way too many TV shows.

"Can I go in while you keep looking? My assistant is motioning to me, and I want to start checking on the patients." Daniel and Cleo were in there somewhere.

The soldier waved her through, even as he switched on a flashlight and continued looking.

"Tracy…" Ben, forced to wait for his vehicle to pass inspection, gave her a warning growl, but she shrugged him off.

"I'll meet you once you get through the checkpoint. Don't let them confiscate the antibiotics."

And with that, she made her escape. Securing her mask and feeling guilty, she stepped around the line of military vehicles and met Pedro, pulling him a safe distance away from the soldier who'd stopped him.

"It's pneumonic plague," she whispered, switching to Portuguese while noting he was already wearing a mask. "You'll need to start on antibiotics immediately."

"I thought so. They're staying pretty tight-lipped about

the whole thing, but they've set up a quarantine area. Those who are ill have been kept separate from those who still appear healthy—which aren't many at this point."

"Any more deaths? How are Daniel and Cleo?"

"Who?"

"The two kids we found in the field."

Daniel, the boy she'd taken samples from, had been lying in a grassy area, too weak to stand and walk. His sister, showing signs of the illness as well, had refused to leave his side. They'd carried them back to an empty house, just as the military had shown up and taken over.

"No change in the boy, although there have been two more deaths."

"And Cleo?"

"She's definitely got it, but now that we know what we're dealing with, we can start them both on treatment." Pedro slung his arm around her and squeezed. "Can I say how glad I am to see you? These soldier boys are some scary dudes."

He said the last line in English, using his best American accent, which made Tracy smile. She glanced over at Ben, who was still glowering at her, and her smile died.

The soldiers weren't the only scary dudes.

Pedro continued, "The military docs have IVs going on some of the patients, but they wouldn't tell me what they injected into the lines."

"Strange." She glanced at one of the houses, which currently had a small contingent of guards at the doors and windows. "Did they say anything about antibiotics?"

"I think they're still trying to get a handle on things."

Ben joined them on foot, and she frowned at him. "Where's your car?"

"They're going to drive it in and park it in front of one of the houses. They've evidently got a research area already set up."

He glanced at Pedro, whose arm was still around her, obviously waiting for an introduction. Okay, this was going to be fun. She noticed Pedro also seemed to be assessing Ben, trying to figure out what his place was in all this. He'd never asked about her ring, and she'd never volunteered any information. Several people had assumed she was widowed, and she'd just let it ride. Maybe she could simply omit Ben's relationship to her.

Well, that would be easy enough, because there was no relationship.

"Ben, this is Pedro, my assistant." She hesitated. "Pedro, this is Ben, head epidemiologist at the *Centro de Doenças Tropicais* in Teresina. He's the one I went to see." Maybe no one would notice that she'd conveniently left out his last name. Not that she went by it any more.

Ben held out his hand. "Ben Almeida. Nice to meet you." He slid Tracy a smile that said he knew exactly what she'd done and why. "I also happen to be Tracy's husband."

The look of shock in her assistant's eyes was unmistakable, and he quickly removed his arm from around her shoulders. He shot her a look but dutifully shook hands and muttered something appropriate. She, on the other hand, sent Ben a death stare meant to cut him in two. Instead, he seemed totally unfazed by her ire.

Ben nodded. "I've heard Tracy's account of what happened here. Why don't you tell me what you've observed?"

It was said as if she was clueless. Pressure began building in the back of her head.

Her assistant knew better. "Well, she's probably told you more than I could. We've got about fifteen cases of… Tracy said it's pneumonic plague?"

"Yes." Ben's eyes followed the progress of some men in hazard gear as they went from one building to another. "And judging from the way they're treating it, they know what they're dealing with. Are they still burning the bodies?"

"Yes. Two more in the last couple of hours," Pedro said.

"The boy whose sample I brought in—Daniel—is still alive, but he's pretty sick. His sister is as well."

She didn't need to say what else she knew: antibiotics needed to be started within twenty-four hours of the appearance of symptoms to be effective. Ben would already know that. The treatment window was narrow, but she wouldn't give up, no matter how sick the patient.

Tracy ached for the two children, their mother ripped from them without so much as a funeral service or a chance to say goodbye. Just thrown onto a flaming pyre to destroy any pathogens. How many other kids would watch helplessly as the same thing happened to their relatives? As much as she knew it had to be done, it still didn't make it any easier. How would she feel if the body being burned was Ben's?

No. Not Ben. She wouldn't let her mind go there.

"Where are they putting you up for the night?" she asked Pedro.

"They've got medical civilians in one house and military personnel in another. They post guards out front of both of them, though."

Ben's four-wheel drive pulled up beside them and the soldier poked his head out of the open window. "I'm taking your vehicle to the research center we've set up. Do you want a ride?"

"We'll follow on foot," Ben said. Tracy got the idea, he wanted to continue their conversation in private. "And if you could put Dr. Hinton in the same house as me, I'd appreciate it. I haven't seen my wife in quite a while and would like some alone time with her if possible." He quirked an eyebrow at the man, while reaching over and taking her hand in his and giving it a warning squeeze. The presumption of his move made the rising pressure in her head grow to dangerous levels.

Her poor assistant squirmed visibly.

If Pedro hadn't been beside them, she'd have made it plain how little contact—of any sort—she wanted with him. But she knew Ben well enough to know he didn't say or do anything without a good reason.

The driver grinned and promised to see what he could do.

But, oh, she was going to let Ben know she was *not* happy with that arrangement. She hadn't wanted anyone to know what their relationship was, and now everyone in town would be snickering behind their backs.

"Nice work," she hissed.

Pedro shifted from foot to foot. "I'm sorry, I had no idea you were… I just assumed you were…"

"Single?" Ben supplied, an edge to his voice.

Wow, was he actually doing this? He'd never expressed any hint of jealousy when they'd been together. And she didn't appreciate it now.

"No, not exactly. I just knew she didn't have anyone living with her."

Ben's brows lifted. "You knew that for a fact, did you?"

"Well, yes. W-we had staff meetings at her house on a regular basis."

Tracy took a closer look at her assistant's face. There was discomfiture and something else lurking in his brown eyes. Oh God. Surely he wasn't interested in her. She'd never given him any reason to think she might be remotely attracted to him.

At least, she hoped she hadn't. And yet Ben had automatically assumed Pedro might have his eye on her. Why would he even care?

She touched Pedro's arm. "Ben and I…well, it's complicated."

Complicated. It was. At least for her. And Ben had probably never forgiven her for walking away from their marriage without a word. But what could she have said, really?

Not only do I not want to get pregnant again, I might choose to have my non-cancerous breasts removed.

She could still explain, if she wanted to. But after the way he'd run roughshod over her four years ago, going behind her back and manipulating her into coming home, he'd pretty much snuffed out any feelings of guilt on her part.

Ben had been part of the reason she'd struggled with making a final decision about what to do about her test results. But now that he and the baby were no longer part of the equation, she'd put things on hold, choosing to make a difference in the lives of others instead.

Dragging her attention back to Pedro, she tried her best to finish her earlier statement. Putting more emphasis on the words than was strictly necessary, she wanted to make sure she got her point across to both of them.

"Ben and I are separated. We have been for quite some time. So anything that happens between us will be strictly business."

Now, if she could just convince herself of that, she should be good to go.

CHAPTER FIVE

THERE WAS A reason it was called the Black Death.

There was nothing pretty or romantic about the plague. And the pneumonic form of the disease was the most dangerous, rapidly killing those it touched.

Ben stepped into the tiny house where the patients were being housed, and he fought a wave of pure desolation as he looked over the place. Tracy seemed just as shocked, standing motionless in the doorway beside her assistant.

Simple green cots were packed into what used to be a living room, laid out in two rows with barely enough space between beds for doctors to work.

Ben counted silently. Fourteen patients. And not all of them had IVs started. In fact, when he looked closer, he saw that the wall over some of the cots had a crude "X" penned in black ink.

A chill went over him. Deathbeds.

His gaze moved further and he spotted two men he assumed were doctors, still wearing that hazard gear he'd spotted earlier. The pair stood on either side of a bed, assessing a woman who was wailing, the sound coming in fits and starts that were interrupted by coughing spasms. One of the men leaned past the patient and slashed a mark over the bed.

Just like that. Bile pumped into his stomach in a flood.

Tracy's gaze met his, her eyes reflecting pure horror. She reached out and gripped Pedro's sleeve. "So many."

The man nodded. "I know."

None of the trio had on the protective clothing worn by the other doctors, other than masks and latex gloves, but as Tracy was on antibiotics and Pedro had just been given his first dose, there was no need. He assumed the heavy gear worn by the other men would be done away with pretty soon.

Besides, it was stifling in the room, the number of bodies cranking up the temperatures to unbearable levels. There wasn't even a fan to move the air around, probably out of fear of microbes being carried outside the room. But none of these patients—even the ones without the fatal mark on the wall—would last long if they couldn't cool it down.

Ben decided that one of his first orders of business would be to set up some kind of misting system.

Tracy moved towards him and touched his arm, pointing to the left at a nearby patient. It was a boy who Ben assumed was the one she'd been so worried about. There was a black squiggle over his bed but it was incomplete, as if someone had started to cross him off the list of the living and had then changed his mind.

"I'm going to check on Daniel and Cleo."

Pedro made a move to follow then noticed Ben's frown and evidently thought better of it, shifting his attention to a patient on the other side of the room instead.

Why did he care if the man had a thing for Tracy? Unlike him, the assistant seemed to have no problem with her job. He probably traveled with her every chance he got.

A steady pain thumped on either side of his head, and he squeezed the bridge of his nose in an effort to interrupt the nerve impulses.

While Tracy checked on the boy, he made his way to

the suited pair across the room. He identified himself and flashed his ID card, causing one of the men's brows to lift. "You're the *epidemiologista* General Gutierrez sent for?"

Ben nodded. "Are you marking these beds on his orders?"

"Well, no. He won't be here until tomorrow." They glanced quickly at each other. "But we can't take care of fourteen patients on our own, so we've been…" The words trailed away, but Ben understood. They were deciding who was worth their care and who was beyond saving.

"Well, Dr. Hinton and myself will be joining you, so let's set up a rotating schedule. Between all of us I'm sure we can make an effort to see *all* the patients." He let his emphasis hang in the air.

"But some of them won't last a day."

"And some of them might," he countered. "Why don't you explain to me who you've assessed, and we'll divide the room into critical care and non-critical, just like you would for field triage. It'll help us divide our efforts."

Neither man looked happy to be challenged, but they didn't contradict him either. If he knew General Gutierrez, the man had told them to follow his recommendations. The doctors gave him a quick rundown and Ben made a list, marking "TI"—for *tratamento intensivo*—next to those patients who were in critical condition and needed extra care. Not one "X" went next to anyone's name.

Ben moved over to the older woman who'd cried out as the men had marked her bed and found she was indeed critical, with red staining around her mouth that signaled she was producing bloody sputum. He laid a gloved hand on her forehead and spoke softly to her, her glassy eyes coming up to meet his, even as her breath rasped in and out, breathing labored. "We're going to take good care of you, okay?"

She blinked at him, not even making an effort to speak.

Ben called out to Tracy. "I want IVs started on all the patients who don't currently have one. We're going to push antibiotics into them. All of them." Then he turned to one of the men and nodded towards the radio on his hip. "Can you get me General Gutierrez? He and I need to have a little chat."

She didn't know what he'd done, but Ben had obviously spoken to someone in authority and asked for some changes. The cots—with the help of other soldiers—had been rearranged according to how ill each patient was. Daniel and Cleo had ended up on opposite sides of the room.

Heart aching, she moved from the boy to another patient, trying not to think about his prospects as she quickly filled a syringe from a vial of antibiotics and inserted it into the injection port of the IV line, marking the time and amounts in a small spiral-bound notebook they'd made up for each patient.

She caught Pedro's eye from across the room and smiled.

"You doing okay?" she mouthed, receiving a thumbs-up in return. Although not a doctor, Pedro had accompanied her on many of her forays into villages and had helped enough that she knew he could hold his own in an emergency. She also trusted him enough to know he'd ask for help if something was beyond his capabilities.

Her shirt was soaked with sweat and she'd gone through masks at an alarming rate. She hoped Ben had brought a big supply. He'd mentioned setting up a rudimentary misting system to help cool off the room.

Right now, though, he was seeing to the unloading of his car, and she refused to think about where they were going to sleep tonight. Ben had said the same "house"… not the same "room" when he'd made his request. But he'd also made it plain that they were married, so she had no doubt they'd be placed together. What was he thinking? Surely he had no more desire to be with her than she had to be with him?

Okay, maybe "desire" was the wrong word to use. Because put them in a room alone together and they tended to combust at frightening speed. She remembered her fury as she'd walked into that village to confront him on their first meeting. She'd heard there was an epidemiologist heading her way down the river but that he was taking his sweet time.

Unwilling to wait for him to stop at every village and sample the local cuisine, she'd powered back upriver and stomped her way to the heart of the village. He'd been standing in the middle of a group of men, a big smile on his face. She'd opened her mouth to throw a vile accusation his way, only to have the words stop in her throat the second their eyes had met.

He'd stared at her for several long seconds then one eyebrow had quirked upwards. "Are you here for me?"

"I...I..." Realizing she'd looked like a fool, she'd drawn herself up to her full height and let him have it.

She'd let him have it again two days later. In an entirely different way.

Oh, God. She could *not* be in a room alone with the man if she could help it. So what was she going to do?

Stay with her patients as much as possible, that's what. She'd already been here for almost eight hours. And it was now a few minutes past the end of her shift. If she knew Ben, he would make them all stick to the schedule he'd drawn up—whether they wanted to or not.

Even as she thought it, she reached Cleo's bed and leaned over her. The girl gave her a tremulous smile, which she returned.

"Hey, how are you doing?"

"Sleepy, and my head hurts." Cleo's voice was a thread of sound.

"I know." Headaches were one of the symptoms of the plague, but Cleo's episode didn't seem to be progressing as rapidly as Daniel's had. "You need to rest. I'm sure—"

Something cool and moist hit her left ankle and swept up the back of her leg until it reached the bottom of her shorts. Stifling a scream, she straightened and spun around to find empty air. She lowered her gaze and spied Ben, on his haunches, about a foot away, a spray bottle in his hand. Half-thought words bubbled on her tongue but didn't find an exit.

He got two more squirts in before she found her voice. "What do you think you're doing?"

Holding the pump bottle up, he said. "We have a room full of sick people. All we need is to have a dengue outbreak on top of everything."

Repellant. Ah. She got it.

But why was he the one spraying it on her? He could have just handed her the bottle and ordered her to put it on.

"You were busy," he said, as if reading her thoughts. "And sometimes with you it's easier to act than to argue."

Like their first kiss? When he'd dragged her to him and planted his lips on hers without so much as a "May I?"

She swallowed, hoping he couldn't read the direction of her thoughts. Or the fact that seeing him kneeling in front of her reminded her of other times when he'd done just that.

Before she could grab the bottle out of his hand he went back to work and sprayed the front of her legs. "Turn around."

"Are you going to personally spray Pedro and the other workers, too? Or just me?"

"They're not wearing shorts." His brows went up. "Didn't think it was as urgent."

She couldn't stop the smile or the roll of her eyes, but

she obediently turned around. In reality the chill of the spray against her super-heated skin was heavenly as he slowly misted the back of her right leg. Looking down, she found Cleo looking up at her.

"He's bossy," the little girl said. Her voice was weak but there was a ghost of a smile on her face.

Tracy couldn't stop the laugh that bubbled out, her heart lightening at Cleo's ability to joke. "Oh, honey, you have no idea."

Ben's bossiness had a tendency to come out in all kinds of ways. Some of those she was better off not thinking about right now.

The spraying stopped and Tracy glanced behind her to find Ben staring up at her. Standing abruptly, he shoved the repellant bottle into her hands. "I'll let you finish up the rest. Give it to the other workers after you're done. And make sure you stay protected while you're here."

With that he walked away without a backward glance.

Stay protected? With him in the immediate vicinity?

She gave a huge sigh.

It would take a whole lot more than a bottle of repellent to do that.

CHAPTER SIX

He was a masochist.

Ben stared at the figure sleeping in the hammock—her back to him—and wondered what on earth he'd been thinking by demanding they sleep in the same room. He obviously hadn't been thinking at all, but the sight of Tracy standing next to Pedro had sent a shaft of what could only be described as jealousy through him.

Why?

She could have been sleeping with twenty men a day after she'd left, and he'd have been none the wiser.

Yeah, but he hadn't had to stand there and witness it.

Even as he tried to convince himself that was the reason, he knew it went deeper than that. Deeper than the desire that churned to life as he stared at the sexy curve of hip flowing into a narrow waist. A waist that hadn't even had time to expand much before their baby had been lost.

She'd gotten off work two hours ahead of him, just as his schedule had dictated, which was a relief because she'd obviously come right back to the room and gone straight to sleep.

Which was exactly what he should be doing.

Tomorrow was going to be just as difficult as today.

Having Tracy here brought up all the tangled emotions he thought he'd already unraveled and put to bed. Sighing, he toed off his shoes, glad he'd donned a pair of athletic shorts to sleep in, because there was no way he was sleeping in just his boxers.

He slid into his hammock, trying to keep the creaking of the ropes to a minimum as he settled into place.

Someone like Pedro would have been ideal husband material for Tracy. He obviously didn't mind her vagabond spirit. In fact, he traveled with her on a regular basis, if appearances were anything to go by.

But then again, Pedro wasn't married to her. He hadn't had to sit at home wondering why she wanted to be anywhere else but with him. Wondering if, once their child was born, the baby would be dumped in the care of his housekeeper, just as he'd been when he'd been little.

Anger churned in his chest at the thought.

So why had seeing her bending over that little girl's bed, shapely bottom facing him, made the saliva pool in his mouth? And when she'd leaned further over, the long, lean muscles in her calves bunching as she'd gone on tiptoe to adjust the sheet on the far side of the cot, his body had roared to life. There hadn't been a drop of anger in sight.

He'd wanted her. Just as much as he always had.

He'd meant to hand her the bottle of repellent with a brusque order to put some on, but he'd been desperate to erase the images cascading through his mind. Squirting a healthy dose of cold liquid on her had seemed like the ideal way to shock her into moving—and shock his own body back to normal. Like a virtual defibrillator, halting a deadly spiral of electrical impulses before they'd overwhelmed his system.

His actions had backfired, though.

She'd turned around, just like he'd hoped, only his senses hadn't righted themselves, they'd gone berserk. And when he'd heard that low, throaty laugh at something her young patient had said, his stomach had turned inside out, drilling him with the reality of how stupid his move had been.

Besides, he'd had other things he needed to attend to.

Like going out and dunking his head in a bucket of water.

Which he'd done. Literally.

When he'd gone back inside, Tracy had already finished spraying herself down, the shine from the repellant glinting off the tip of her upturned nose, making his gut twist all over again.

He'd spent the rest of the day hanging mosquito netting around all of the patients' beds and caring for the ones who were the farthest away from his ex-wife.

Now, if he could just convince himself she really was his ex, he'd be just peachy.

Only two days into the outbreak and she was dog-tired. And hot.

So terribly hot. And now they were up to twenty patients, rather than fourteen.

The tiny house was still stifling, although Ben had figured out a way to combine fans with periodic jets of fine mist that reminded Tracy of the produce sections she'd seen at US supermarkets. It did help, but still…the place could never be deemed "cool."

Then again, it never really cooled off in this part of the world. Tracy had become soft, working in São Paulo for much of the year. The sticky heat that blanketed the equator—a place where seasons didn't exist—was unrelenting, reaching into every nook and cranny.

It had to be just as hard for Ben, who worked in an air-conditioned office nowadays, rather than doing fieldwork like he'd done when they'd met.

They'd administered a therapeutic dose of antibiotics into all their patients, but they were already seeing the truth of that narrow window of treatment. The patients who'd been diagnosed after help arrived and given antibiotics immediately were doing better than those who had already been ill when they'd arrived.

The statistics held true, with the sickest of their patients continuing their downward spiral. Still, they had to keep trying, so they stayed their course, using either IV antibiotics, intramuscular injections or, for those who could tolerate it, oral doses. Two more had died since their arrival, but at least Ben had ordered those awful marks above the beds to be scrubbed clean.

Amazingly, Daniel—although gravely ill—was still hanging in there.

She glanced over at Ben, who was injecting his next patient, squeezing the woman's hand and offering her an encouraging smile that she couldn't actually see—because of his mask—but the crinkling at the corners of his eyes gave him away. Oh, how Tracy had loved seeing those happy little lines go to work.

He put the syringe into the medical waste container they'd set up, and Tracy reminded herself to check on the supply of disposable needles. He caught her looking at him from her place beside Daniel's bed and made his way over to her. She tensed, just as she'd done every time they'd had to interact.

"Why don't you take a quick nap?"

She shook her head. "I'm okay. Besides, I've had more sleep than you have."

Something she would know, as she'd heard him get up in the middle of the night and leave their room both nights they'd been in there. Maybe he was as restless as she was.

Well, whose fault was that? He'd been the one who'd insisted they stay together, which had made things incredibly awkward with Pedro.

And there were no real beds, so it wasn't a matter of

her getting the bed while he slept on a pallet on the floor. No, all the workers had been assigned military hammocks, the residents' original hammocks having been confiscated, along with most of their fabric or upholstered possessions. Once some of the patients recovered, they'd have the added hardship of knowing many of their household clothes and belongings were long gone. Destroyed for the good of the village.

Tracy, for once, had agreed with the decision when Ben told her about it.

In addition to the bed situation, there wasn't much privacy to be had anywhere in the town. Showers had been set up in a clearing and the stinging smell of strong disinfectant soap had become an all-too-familiar fragrance around the compound. But even that couldn't totally vanquish the warm masculine scent that greeted her each night from the neighboring hammock where Ben lay.

Hanging side by side, the two hammocks were slung on three hooks, sharing one at the lower end, while the two upper ends branched apart onto two separate hooks, so that the hammocks formed a V. Knowing their feet were almost touching each and every night had been part of the reason for her sleeplessness.

So she'd lain awake for hours, despite her growing fatigue, until Ben—like he'd done the previous two nights—had slipped from his bed and out of the room. Only then had she finally been able to close her eyes and relax.

Ben looked like he was about to press his point about her taking a nap when the front door to the house banged open and a fierce argument carried through to where they were standing.

What in the name of...?

Both she and Ben moved quickly into the hallway, not wanting someone to be inadvertently exposed to the sickroom. They found one of the military police who'd been assigned to enforcing the quarantine arguing with a young girl who was around six years old. Tear tracks marked the dust on either side of the child's face, and her feet—clad only in flip-flops—were caked with dirt.

"What's going on?" Ben asked in Portuguese.

"She insists on speaking with a doctor, even though I've explained she can't go in there."

Tracy moved forward. "It's okay. I'll go outside with her."

"Tracy." Ben put a hand on her arm, stopping her.

She sent him a look that she hoped conveyed her irritation. "Someone has to talk to her. Better me than them." She aimed a thumb at the poor soldier.

"You need to at least take off your gear before you go out there."

"I will." She spoke softly to the child, telling her it was okay, that she'd be out in a minute. The girl nodded, the wobbling of her chin as she turned to go wrenching at Tracy's heart.

Ben caught the eye of one of the military doctors and told him they'd be back in a few minutes. They both stripped off their protective gear in the clean area and scrubbed with antibiotic soap. Tracy used her forearm to swipe at her damp forehead, frowning when Ben lifted a hand toward her. She took a quick step back.

"You have suds." He pointed to his own forehead.

She reached up and dabbed it away herself, avoiding his eyes, then pushed through the screen door at the back of the house. They made their way round to the front and the little girl rushed toward them. Ben stepped in front of Tracy, causing her to give a sigh of exasperation. "Ben, please. She's not going to hurt anyone."

Moving around him, she knelt in front of the child. "What's your name?"

"Miriam."

Tracy wanted to gently wipe a smudge on the little girl's forehead, much as Ben had tried to do with her a second ago, but she was too afraid of spreading germs at this point to touch anyone outside the village. "Okay, Miriam. What did you want to tell us?"

"You are doctors?"

"Yes. We both are. It's okay. Is someone sick?"

The girl clasped her hands in front of her and nodded. "My *mami*. She has been ill for two days, but told me not to tell anyone. But now..." Her voice broke on a low sob. "But now she does not wake up, even when I try to feed her broth."

"Where is she?"

"At my house. But it is a long way from here."

The first twinge of alarm filtered up her back. "How far?"

"The next village."

Horrified, Tracy stood in a rush and grabbed Ben's hand, her wide eyes on his. "Could it have spread beyond São João dos Rios?"

No! They'd been so careful, no one had been allowed to leave the village once the military had arrived.

But before that?"

His fingers closed around hers, giving them a quick squeeze, then addressed the child, whose small forehead was now scrunched in distress. "Was your mother coughing?"

"Yes. She said it was just a cold, but I am afraid..." She motioned around the quarantined village. "We have heard what happened here. They say the military is shooting anyone who is sick. I had to sneak past them to find you."

Tracy's heart clenched. She knew how suspicious some of these towns were of government officials. But those fears only helped spread sickness and disease. Because people who were afraid tended to hide things from those who could help them.

Like Tracy had when she'd left Ben four years ago?

No, it wasn't the same thing at all. She forced a smile to her lips, knowing it probably looked anything but reassuring. "No one is shooting anyone."

"Will you come and help my mother, then?"

Tracy glanced at the house, where one of the military police watched them closely. Would they let her travel to the village or would they insist on sending someone else? It was a tough call. She didn't want to risk spreading anything, but the more people involved, the more places the disease could be carried. "Yes, honey, I will."

When she tried to move towards the guard, Ben clamped down on her hand. "What do you think you're doing, Tracy?" he murmured, sending a whisper of air across her cheek that made her shiver.

"You heard her. Her mother is sick."

"You could end up making things worse for everyone."

The shiver turned to ice in her veins. Those words were too close to the message he'd sent with the military four years ago. Her brows went up and she looked pointedly at the guard behind them. "I'm going, whether you approve or not. You could always send your little friends after me. You seem to be quite good at doing that."

"Come on, Tracy. You know why I sent them. You were carrying our child."

She did know—and maybe she'd been foolish to travel alone, but she'd been just six weeks along and she'd already had her yellow fever shot. She also knew her reason for taking off that week had had little to do with the village and everything to do with the results of her test. Even so, the blinding humiliation of seeing those uniformed officials set foot on that beach—and knowing her husband had been behind their presence—still stung.

They glared at each other. The last thing she needed to do right now was antagonize him further. She forced her voice to soften. "Please, try to understand. I *have* to check on her mother. My job is part of what keeps me going."

"Keeps you going?"

That last phrase had slipped out before she realized it. Leave it to Ben to catch it as it flew by.

"I mean, my job is important to me, that's all."

His gaze raked her face, and she held her breath, hoping the raw fear that slithered up her throat wasn't visible. Breaking eye contact, he glanced down at the girl, whose terror was much more on the surface. "Fine. We'll both go. But we need to take precautions. We're on antibiotics, so I'm not worried about us, but I also don't want us carrying anything back that way."

Was that why he'd been worried? Maybe she'd misjudged him.

"What about Miriam?" She kept her voice just as low, switching to English to make it harder for the little girl to understand what she was saying. "They may not let her leave São João dos Rios, now that she's been exposed."

"I know. I'll talk to the guard and get her started on antibiotics."

Poor girl, she had no idea that by trying to get help for her mother she might become a virtual prisoner. And if the worst came to the worst, and her mother had the deadly disease, she might never see her again.

A familiar pang went through Tracy's chest. Her mother had died while Tracy had been here in Brazil. Six months after she and Ben had married, in fact. Her mother had had no idea she was sick during the wedding rehearsal or as they'd planned what should have been a happy occasion. But then she'd been diagnosed a few weeks after the ceremony. She'd died months later.

Squaring her shoulders, she went through the motions

of going with Ben to talk to the guard, who in turn had to make a phone call up his chain of command. An hour later, she, Ben, and four military personnel were on their way to the next village. Ben had his arm around her in the backseat of the four-wheel drive to help steady her as they hit pothole after pothole, the scarred tract rarely seeing much in the way of motor vehicles.

Loaded to the gills with medical equipment, as well as Ben's lab stuff, she leaned against him, allowing him to pull her even closer as she prayed that whatever they found would not be as bad as she feared.

"Bronchitis," Ben declared.

Tracy almost laughed aloud as a giddy sense of relief swept over her. "Are you sure?"

Ben sat behind the house on a low three-legged stool, studying the last of the slides through his microscope.

"I don't see any sign of plague bacteria. And she's awake now. No fever or symptoms other than some thick congestion in her chest." He leaned back and looked at her. "She probably kept going until she was literally worn out, which was why Miriam couldn't wake her up. Regardless, we don't have a case of the plague here."

"Thank God." Her legs threatened to give out, and she had to put a hand on Ben's shoulder to brace herself.

He glanced up at her, concern in his eyes. "Hey, sit down before you fall down." Before she realized what he was doing, he'd pulled her onto his left knee.

"Sorry," he murmured. "There's nowhere else to sit."

She nodded. "I'm sorry about what I said earlier. About you sending the military after me."

"Don't worry about it. You were upset."

She blinked. He'd just given her absolution. Whether it was for sins of the past or sins of the present was immaterial right now—not when the blood was thickening in her veins, the air around her turning crystal clear with secret knowledge.

The sudden sound of his breath being let out and the way his arm tightened around her back were her undoing. All she could think about was that she owed him a huge "thank you." Before she could stop herself, she looped her arms around his neck and leaned forward to kiss him.

CHAPTER SEVEN

HER LIPS GRAZED his cheek.

Ben wasn't at all sure how it happened. First she was apologizing then her mouth was on his skin. The instant it happened, something from the past surged inside him, and he brushed aside the gesture in favor of something a little more personal. If she was going to kiss him, he was going to make damned sure it counted. Using his free hand to cup her head, he eased her round until she faced him.

He stared at her for a long moment, taking in the parted lips, glittering eyes...an expression he knew all too well. He lowered his head, an inner shout of exultation going off in his skull when she didn't flinch away but met him halfway.

Their lips connected, and it was as if a match had been struck in the presence of gasoline fumes. They both went up in flames.

A low moan slid between them. One that most certainly hadn't come from him. Taking that as a signal to continue, his fingers lifted and tunneled deep into her hair, the damp moisture of her scalp feeling cool against his overheated skin.

Ignoring the microscope and slides, he shifted her legs sideways until they rested between his, without breaking contact with her mouth for even a second.

The change in position pressed her thigh against his

already tightening flesh, which was pure torture—made him want to push back to increase the contact. He forced himself to remain still instead, although it just about killed him. It had been four years since he'd held this woman in his arms, and he wasn't about to blow it by doing anything that would have her leaping from his lap in a panic. Realistically, he knew they weren't going to have sex behind the house of an ill woman, but he could take a minute or two to drink his fill of her.

Only, he'd never really get his fill. Would always want more than she was willing to give.

He licked along the seam of her mouth, asking for permission. She granted it without a word, opening to him. He went deep, his hand tightening in her hair as he tipped her head sideways seeking to find the best angle possible. She wiggled closer, taking him almost to the brink before he got himself back under control.

He gave a hard swallow. *Slow.*

Exploring the heat and warmth he found between her lips, he tried to rememorize everything and realized he didn't need to. Because he'd forgotten nothing. Not the taste of her, not the shivers he could wring from her by using his teeth in addition to his tongue.

And when he could no longer contain his low groan, her fingers came up and tangled in his hair. He could feel the battle going on within her and fought against his own need to control the situation, letting her lead instead.

Unfortunately, she took that as a signal to pull back, her breath coming in husky snatches of sound that he found erotic beyond belief.

She took a couple more quick gulps before attempting to talk.

"Ben," she whispered, her mouth still against his. "What are we doing here?"

In spite of himself, he smiled. "I thought that was fairly obvious."

"Mmm." The hum of sound drove him crazy, just like it always had. "This is a mistake. You know it is."

"I know." He bit her lower lip, sucking on the soft flesh before releasing it with a growl. "Doesn't mean I didn't enjoy it, though. Or that you didn't either."

"I know." No arguments, no denying that she felt the same. Just an acknowledgement of what was obvious to both of them.

It had been an incredibly long week, and all he wanted to do was wrap his arms around her, make slow, satisfying love and then go to sleep still trapped inside her. Just like they used to.

But he knew that was the exhaustion talking. Not to mention that thing wedged against her hip, which was busy shouting out commands he was doing his best to ignore.

Sorry, bud. You're out of luck.

Tracy leaned her forehead against his and gave a drawn-out sigh. "We need to get back to the other village if this one is in the clear."

She heaved one more sigh, before climbing to her feet, looking anywhere but at his lap, which was probably smart. "I'm sure we're both so tired we're not thinking straight. We'll regret this once we've had some sleep."

She might, but he wouldn't. Not even if he slept as long as Rip Van Winkle. He'd still wake up and want to kiss her all over again.

He closed his eyes for a long moment then started undoing his equipment without a word.

She laid a hand on his shoulder. "If it's any consolation, you're right. I enjoyed it too. You always were a great kisser."

Some of the tension in his spine seeped away. Questions from four years ago resurfaced and he couldn't keep himself from asking, "Then why were you always in such a hurry to leave?"

"Please, don't, Ben. Not right now."

And her response was exactly the same as it had been back then. She hadn't wanted to talk about it—had just wanted to head off on her next adventure.

There was nothing left to say, then. "I'll get some medicine out of the car and explain the dosage."

She nodded. "I'm sure they'll even let Miriam come home as there's no evidence of pneumonic plague here. We'll put her on the prophylactic dosage of antibiotics and she should be fine."

Stowing his equipment in a large box and carefully stacking his microscope on top, all he could do was wish for a prophylactic dose of something that would cut through his current jumble of emotions and put him back on the road to normalcy.

Normalcy. Wow. If he ever found a pill that would restore that, he'd end up a very rich man.

Tracy could have kicked herself. She'd let him kiss her. *On the mouth.* Worse, she'd kissed him back. Crazily. As if she couldn't get enough of him.

Her chaste little gesture of thanks had flared to inferno proportions in a nanosecond.

The chemistry between them was just as potent as ever. Something she never should've doubted. Something she should have been braced for and never allowed to happen.

And why on earth had she let herself be drawn into an argument about the past? Because she was trying to keep her distance emotionally? You sure couldn't tell it from where she stood. Because the only message she'd been sending while perched on his lap had been more along the lines of throw-me-on-my-back-and-take-me-hard.

To allow that to happen, though, would only make

things more complicated. Especially now. She could admit that she still cared about him, but it didn't mean they could—or should—be together. If she thought there was a chance, she might try to explain what had happened all those years ago. But it wouldn't do any good at this point. And the last thing she needed was Ben's pity. Hanging onto the anger from the past might be best for both of them right now, because in another week or so they'd be heading in opposite directions.

Lying in her hammock, hours from the time they'd finally climbed into Ben's SUV and headed back to town, she still longed to reach across the space and take his hand. Touch his face. Kiss his lips.

Why? None of it made any sense.

There were less than two feet separating them. Less at the foot end of the hammocks. And she'd never been more keenly aware of that fact than she was now. The village was still and quiet. The military doctors had taken up the night shift, leaving Tracy and Ben to get five or six hours of sleep, which was what she should be doing right now, rather than lying here staring at the ceiling. Luckily, Ben was facing away from her and couldn't see her restless movements. He'd fallen asleep almost as soon as his body had hit the hammock, while she'd pretended to do the same. Was still pretending, in fact.

Just like she'd pretended that kiss today was the result of exhaustion and stress.

He turned unexpectedly, and Tracy clamped her eyelids shut, trying to breathe slowly and deeply, even though her heart was pounding out a crazy tattoo. The sound of a throat clearing, some more rustling and then a low, exasperated curse met her ears. She felt a rush of air against her and the movement of his hammock disturbing hers where they intersected at the bottom.

Soft footsteps. Another oath. Then the sound of a door quietly opening and closing. Just like the last three nights.

She waited for several seconds before she got up the courage to open her eyes again and peek.

Yep. He was gone. Where was he disappearing to each night? The restroom? If so, that meant he'd be back in a matter of minutes—which he never was. She pushed her fingers through the open-weave fabric of her hammock in irritation, squeezing the fibers tight. Instead of wondering where he was, she should be using this time to try to go to sleep.

Fat chance of that now.

She continued to lie very still, waiting, staring at the closed door on the other side of the tiny room.

But fifteen minutes later there was still no sign of him, just like on previous nights. Had he decided he couldn't sleep? Yes, it was hot in the room—the fan doing nothing more than fluffing the balmy air—but it would be just as hot no matter where he went.

Did this have something to do with their kiss, earlier? If that were the case, then what was his excuse on the other nights?

Crossing her arms over her chest, she closed her eyes again and tried for the umpteenth time to go to sleep. Morning was going to come, and with it a whole new day of struggles and trials as they tried to care for their remaining patients.

Seven more days. That's how long Ben figured it would take to get the epidemic under control.

And that's how long she had to kick this stupid attraction to the curb and keep herself out of Ben's bed.

Seven, very long days.

CHAPTER EIGHT

"CLEO'S RIGHT HERE, honey."

Gently placing a moist cloth across Daniel's feverish brow, Tracy nodded at the neighboring cot, where Ben was adjusting the IV pole.

The boy had finally regained consciousness, four days after being found in the field. His first words had been to ask about his sister. The plea had remained throughout the day, sometimes interrupted by bouts of coughing, sometimes gasped between harsh breaths, but he never relented. The question was there each time he rallied for a few moments. And it made Tracy's heart squeeze. It was as if, even in his precarious state, he refused to believe Cleo was alive unless he saw it for himself.

Ben had finally relented and offered to shuffle patients around so that the brother and sister could remain close to each other's sides, despite the fact that he'd wanted patients placed according to severity of illness. Daniel was still gravely ill, whereas Cleo's sickness had not ravaged her young body as much as those of some of their other patients. She said her head still ached, but she hadn't worsened.

Daniel's glassy eyes swiveled to the right. "Clee," he whispered, shaky fingers reaching across the space and then dropping before he succeeded in reaching the other bed.

"She's here, Daniel, but she's asleep right now. We have to let her rest so she can be strong and healthy again." Her gloved fingers brushed back a moist lock of hair, a rush of emotion clogging her throat. "You need to do the same. She'll still be here when you wake up."

If you wake up.

She immediately dismissed the thought. Daniel's vitals had slowly grown weaker over the last couple of days, but he continued to fight harder than anyone she'd ever seen. And so would she. She'd come here to fight for these kids, against the military's wishes…against Ben's wishes. And she was going to damn well keep on fighting.

Maybe there was a message for her in there somewhere. But she was too tired to dig for it right now. Maybe later.

As if he sensed the direction of her thoughts, Ben came to stand beside her. "You need to get some rest as well. You look exhausted."

"We're all tired." She reached up to wipe a trickle of perspiration from her temple only to have Ben beat her to it, using one of the dry compresses to blot her forehead. She gave him a weak grin. "You'd think after almost a week I'd be used to the heat. I travel down the Amazon all the time."

They both froze, and Tracy wondered if he was remembering that last fateful trip.

Ben had accused her of neglecting their marriage, of being careless with their baby's health. Had she? Had her own plight so blinded her that she'd taken unnecessary chances?

She'd never know. And there was nothing she could do to go back and change things anyway.

Guilt gnawed at her, just as strong now as it had been back then.

"You're good with them, you know."

The change in subject made her blink. "With who?"

He nodded toward the kids. "These two."

"I care about all my patients."

"I wasn't accusing you of anything, Tracy. Just making a statement."

She considered that for a moment. The anger had been so strong at the end of their marriage that it was hard to hear anything he said without the filters of the past. Maybe she should start trying to take his words at face value. Maybe he could start doing the same.

She perched on the side of Cleo's bed, her fingers feathering through the girl's hair. A low sigh came from the child's throat, and she snuggled into her hand.

Tears pricked very close to the surface but she ignored them as best she could. "I can't imagine how they're going to feel when they wake up and realize their mother is gone. For ever."

Well, she took that back. She knew how that felt but she'd at least had her mom with her until she was a grown woman. These kids would never know how that felt. She wished there was some way she could take that pain from them.

"Sometimes a parent doesn't have to die to be gone," Ben murmured.

She glanced up at him, but he was staring through the dusty window across from them.

"Are you talking about your mom and dad?" Ben and Marcelo's parents hadn't been around much as they'd been growing up and both men carried some resentment about that. That resentment had carried over to Ben's marriage.

Her traveling had been a constant source of arguments almost from the moment they'd both said, "I do."

But Ben had been just as gung ho about his job when they'd met. She hadn't understood exactly why he'd wanted to give all that up. Well, that wasn't quite true either. When she'd found out she was pregnant, she'd been all set to let her office take over a lot of *Projeto Vida's* off-site calls. Then things had changed.

And Ben had reacted badly to her need for space...for time to think. In reality, she probably should have told him sooner, but she'd still been reeling from the news and grieving over her mother's and sisters' deaths.

Ben's eyes refocused on her. "No. Just talking in generalities."

He was lying. But it was easier to let this particular subject go. "I forgot to ask. How's Rosa?"

"Fine. Still at the house."

She wasn't surprised. The old housekeeper—who'd been widowed at a young age and had never remarried—had practically raised Ben and Marcelo. Of course Ben would keep her on. It was another thing they'd argued about.

Oh, not about Rosa still living there—Tracy loved her almost as much as Ben—but that he wouldn't hear of the housekeeper having any part in raising their child. The early elation of finding out she was pregnant hadn't lasted long.

When he'd asked about her plans for her job once the baby was born, she'd flippantly responded that Rosa would be thrilled to help during her absences—that she'd already asked her, in fact. Her words had been met with stony silence. Seconds later Ben had stalked from the room and slammed through the front door of the house.

Only afterwards had she realized how her comment might have sounded. She'd apologized and tried to explain once he'd come home, but she'd got the feeling Ben had heard little or nothing of what she'd said.

She sighed. "I miss Rosa."

"I'm sure she misses you as well."

Her heart aching, a silent question echoing inside her head: *And what about you, Ben? Do you ever miss me?*

"Don't move too quickly. You're still weak."

Tracy put her shoulder beneath Daniel's arm and, with Pedro on his other side, they helped him walk slowly around the clearing in front of the house in an effort to ward off the possibility of deep vein thromboses from all his time in bed. Day five, and the patient who'd set off the frantic race to save a village seemed to have turned a corner—against all odds. Just yesterday they'd wondered if he would even make it. Somehow the twelve-year-old's body was fighting off the disease when by most medical journals' estimations he should be dead.

"M-my sister?" His voice was thin and raspy.

"Cleo is at the cafeteria. You have some catching up to do, you know," she teased. "Do you think you can handle the thought of sipping some broth?"

"I'd rather have *beijú*."

The local flatbread made from cassava flour was typical up here in the northeastern part of the country. Tracy had missed the gummy bread in São Paulo, although she could still find it on occasion.

Pedro shook his head. "I think we'd better stick to broth for today, like Tracy said."

Daniel made a face. "Not even beans and rice?"

"Soon," Tracy said with a smile. "Maybe in another day or two, okay?"

His already thin shoulders slumped, but he didn't argue as they led him over to the temporary mess hall the military had set up. The tent was divided into sides. Medical personnel and healthy villagers on one side and those with active infections on the other. Donning her mask, she ducked beneath the canvas door flap to deliver her patient.

Four long tables with wooden benches were mostly empty. There weren't very many patients at the moment who were well enough to actually walk the short distance from their beds. Huge fans sucked heat from the inside and blew it out, keeping the place from turning into an inferno as the sun baked the canvas roof. In fact, more of the flaps were open today, a sign the military knew things were looking up for the stricken town.

A wave from across the space caught her eye.

Cleo, seated at a front table, smiled, her dark eyes lighting up as she saw them come in. "Daniel, you're awake!" She motioned him over.

Tracy delivered their charge to the table and brother and sister were reunited—outside the sickroom—for the first time in over a week. Cleo's smile wavered and then she wrapped her arms around Daniel's neck and sobbed quietly. Tracy was forced to separate them gently when she grew concerned about the boy's system being overloaded. Before she could ask the person in charge of meals for a cup of broth, one magically appeared on the table in front of them.

Cleo, who'd begun to recover more quickly than Daniel, had black beans and rice on her plate—and Tracy could swear that was a piece of fried banana as well. Her own mouth watered, so she could only imagine how Daniel felt. But he dutifully picked up his spoon and gave a tentative taste of the contents of his cup. Despite the liquid diet, he closed his eyes as if it were the finest caviar.

"Good?" she asked.

He nodded, taking another sip.

Pedro glanced at the serving area. "I'm going to head over and get in line before it closes. What do you want?"

"I already have Tracy's food."

The voice came from behind them just as a tray was plonked down in front of her. A creamy-white *beijú*, slathered in butter, was folded in half and propped up on a neat mound of rice and beans. And, oh! A *whole* fried banana.

"Not fair," muttered Daniel, who looked longingly at the plate and sucked down another spoonful of his broth.

She glanced to the side and saw Ben, his eyes on Pedro as he set down a second tray beside hers. She gave her assistant an apologetic shrug. "Get something before they run out. I'll see you later, okay?"

Ben waited for her to sit before joining her. Irritated, she realized she'd been looking for him all day.

"You're supposed to be on the doctors' side of the tent, you know," she said, cringing as the words left her mouth. Great. No "Thank you" for the food. No "How are you?" Just a veiled accusation.

"Hmm. Well, so should you. I saw you come in and thought you might like an update on our situation."

Our situation?

Oh, he meant here in town. He wasn't referring to that disastrous kiss.

"Is that where you've been? With the military?"

"The guys in charge wanted me to fill them in. General Gutierrez is here and heard most of the news from his own doctors, but he wanted to make sure it matched the civilian report. The military's reputation tends to be a touchy subject."

"Since when?" As soon as the words were out of her mouth she wished she could call them back. "Sorry. That hadn't come out right."

He ignored her and leaned around her back to lay a hand on Daniel's shoulder, smiling at the boy. "I'm surprised to see you out of bed."

Cleo blinked at him with huge brown eyes. "What about me? Are you surprised to see me, too?"

"Definitely. But very glad." He then ruffled Cleo's hair, which caused the seven-year-old to giggle. The happy sound made Tracy's heart contract. The man was a natural with children. He should have lots of them. All swarming around him like a litter of cute puppies.

"I haven't heard a peep about any so-called meetings. Why didn't someone call me?" She wasn't really peeved but needed to get her mind off Ben and his future children.

Because it hurt too much to think about it. Not when she'd decided her previous pregnancy would probably be her last.

He glanced away. "I wanted to let you sleep in a little while longer. It's been a difficult week."

Come to think of it, no one *had* come to wake her up for her normal seven a.m. shift. Had that been Ben's doing as well? Her heart tightened further.

He was a good man. He'd deserved so much better than what she'd given him.

She cleared her throat, trying to get rid of the lump that clogged it. "Thank you. You weren't there when I woke up."

Turning to look at her, he lifted a shoulder. "I'm an early riser. Always have been."

Yes, he had been. But he hadn't normally left their bed in the middle of the night and not returned. A thought came to her. Maybe he'd found somewhere else to hole up. A streak of something white hot went through her. She had noticed a couple of female soldiers eyeing him. But surely…

Daniel lifted the last spoonful of broth and leaned back with a tired sigh.

She wanted to know what had been said during the meeting but she also needed to take care of her patients' needs. "Are you guys ready to go back to your room?"

Ben frowned down at her untouched tray, while Daniel shook his head. "Can I please stay here for a little while longer? I'm tired of lying in bed, and I want to talk to Cleo."

There was a sad note in the words, and Tracy had a feeling she knew what he wanted to talk to her about. What were these kids going to do when this was all over? A thought that had plagued her repeatedly over the past couple of days.

She nodded. "We'll move to another table and give you

some time alone, okay? If you need me, just wave, and I'll see you."

She and Ben picked up their trays. She noticed he headed for a different table than Pedro's. Thankfully her assistant was busy talking to one of the military doctors. Maybe he wouldn't notice.

She realized she wasn't the only one who hadn't touched her plate. "Eat. Then I want to hear about what went on at the meeting."

He lifted his brows. "I'll eat if you will."

Her lips curled into a reluctant smile, and she realized how little of that she'd done over the last week. "Deal."

The next fifteen minutes were spent in relative silence as she enjoyed her first quiet meal since they'd arrived. When she bit into her *beijú* she couldn't stop a low groan of pleasure. Ben remembered exactly how much butter she liked on it. And even though the bread was no longer warm, it was still as good as she remembered. "I have to take some cassava flour back with me so I can make this at home."

Ben didn't respond, and she only realized how that sounded when she noticed a muscle working in his jaw. Surely he knew she'd have to go back to São Paulo soon. Their life together was over, no matter how much she might wish otherwise.

Shaking off her regrets, she forced her back to straighten. "So, how did things go this morning?"

Cutting a chunk of fried banana and popping it into her mouth, she waited for him to fill her in.

"Tell me something," he said instead.

Her whole body went on alert. Because it was he who was supposed to be telling *her* something, not the other way around. And if he asked her about her reasons for leaving, she had no idea what she was going to say. Because for all her raging about Ben's ridiculous actions in sending in the cavalry when she hadn't been in any real danger, she knew it was only a symptom of an underlying problem.

Yes, he'd betrayed her. Yes, he should have come himself, instead of pretending the military had other reasons for her not being in that village. But her reasons for leaving were way more complex than that. Because in the same way the townsfolk's coughs were only a symptom of a raging wildfire burning below the surface, so were her issues.

"I thought we were going to talk about your meeting."

If she thought she could change the subject that easily, she was wrong.

"Why haven't you filed for divorce? Surely you could meet someone who loves your job just as much as you do." His glance went to the table where Pedro sat.

"I—I told you. It's hard to get a divorce from inside Brazil."

"And you mean to tell me that after four years there's been no one you've wanted to spend your life with?"

"If you're talking about Pedro, we're just coworkers." After Ben, she'd wanted no one. "I just haven't had the time to file the paperwork. It would mean a trip to New York."

She tried to turn the conversation back to him. And realized she really did want to know. "What about you?"

"I have no desire to go down that road again."

A spike of guilt went through her heart. Had she done that to him? Been such an awful wife that he'd never consider marrying again? She'd just assumed he'd be happier once she was out of his life, that he'd find someone who could give him what she didn't seem able to. "I see. But surely someday…"

"I don't think so." He dropped his utensils onto his plate with a clatter.

Surely he couldn't kiss her like he'd done a few days ago and not want that with someone else.

"You'd have eventually hated me, Ben. We both know

that. It was better that I left." Defective gene or no defective gene, she and Ben had never seen eye to eye on her job.

But would she have traveled as much without that fear prodding her from behind?

He turned to face her. "I never hated you, Tracy. But I deserved better than a letter left on my desk."

He was right. She'd left him an ugly, anger-filled missive detailing everything about their marriage she found unbearable, ending with the military invasion of the village that had ended in her expulsion. Part of that rage had been due to feelings of helplessness over her test results. Part of it had been caused by grief over the loss of her child. But the biggest part of it had been guilt at having failed him so terribly. She'd been too much of a coward to stick around and tell him to his face that it was over.

"You're right, Ben. It won't help, but I was dealing with something more than my pregnancy at that time."

"Something about your job?"

"No." It was on the tip of her tongue to tell him when Daniel waved from across the room. She realized this was neither the time nor the place to dredge up issues from the past. Not when there were lives in the balance and patients who needed her. "I have to go. I can't change the way things played out, Ben. All I can say is I'm sorry."

"Yeah, well, so am I." Before she could even get up from her place, Ben was already on his feet—had already picked up both their trays and was striding towards the front of the tent where the trashcans were located.

As she went over to Daniel's table, she realized Ben had never told her what the meeting this morning had been about.

And right now she didn't care.

CHAPTER NINE

THEY'D LOST ANOTHER patient during the night, and now this.

A flash of anger went through Tracy's eyes. "We have to stay for a week *after* the last patient recovers? You've got to be kidding. I can't be gone from my job for that long."

Her job. That's what it always came down to.

Unless it was more than that. She'd talked about dealing with other issues during their marriage that had nothing to do with her job. Or her pregnancy. He'd racked his brains, thinking back over every last detail he could remember.

And had come up blank.

Except for a vivid image of that kiss in the neighboring town a few days ago. He couldn't seem to get it out of his head.

In fact, the memory haunted him night after night and infected his dreams. The dreams that drove him from his bed and into the narrow hallway just outside the door. His back was killing him, but it was better than the other part of his body that was also killing him.

"The army is worried about keeping the disease contained, so they're upping the quarantine time." He frowned. "And because we traveled to that neighboring village, they want to keep tabs on it as well and make sure no one starts exhibiting symptoms."

She glanced around the sickroom at the dwindling number of patients. "We'll be sitting here alone, twiddling our thumbs, by that time, and you know it."

More than half of the surviving patients had gone on to recover, and the ones who'd shown no symptoms at all were still on doses of antibiotics and would be for several more days. She was right, though. Once the remaining cases were under control, there'd be no more risk of person-to-person contamination. And they'd be stuck here for a week with nothing to do.

Tracy walked over to one of the patients and checked the IV bag, making sure it didn't need changing. "We wore masks while we were at the other village, Ben."

"Not the whole time."

He saw from the change in her expression that she knew exactly when they'd gone without wearing their protective masks. Right before—and during—that deadly kiss.

She lowered her voice, even though she was speaking in English and no one would understand her. "No one saw us."

"Someone did." He nodded when her eyes widened. "And they reported it to the general."

"I thought you guys were big buddies."

"We're friends. But he's also a stickler for the rules."

"I found that out the hard way." Her eyes narrowed. "Listen, I can't stay here for ever. I have no cellphone reception, and there's no way I can get word back to *Projeto Vida* that I'll be delayed even longer. They need to at least let Pedro head back to the office."

He sighed. They hadn't seen much of Tracy's assistant since lunch the other day, and he wondered if the other man was actively avoiding them. Then again, why would he? Ben's lack of sleep was obviously catching up with him.

"They're not letting anyone out, and I wouldn't try to press the issue, if I were you."

"Did you set this up?"

"Get over yourself, Trace. This has nothing to do with you. Or me, for that matter."

She closed her eyes for a second. "You're right. Sorry."

He thought she actually might be. "Maybe I can ask him to get in touch with your office. I'm sure they must have a satellite phone or something they're using for communication."

Moving over to stand beside her, he touched her hand. "Listen, I know this hasn't been easy. Maybe I shouldn't have let you come in the first place, I don't know. But I'm really not trying to manipulate the situation or make things more difficult than they have to be. It's just as inconvenient for me to be stuck here as it is for you. I have my lab—my own responsibilities. Mandy can't hold down the fort for ever."

Her gaze softened. "Don't think I don't appreciate being able to come, Ben. I do." She hesitated then wrapped her fingers around his. "It just feels…awkward. And I know this is just as hard for you as it is for me. I really am sorry."

When she started to withdraw, he tightened his fingers, holding her in place. "Whatever else happens, it's been good seeing you again." The words had come out before he could stop them, and he could tell by her sharp intake of breath they'd taken her by surprise.

"You too."

Then what were those other issues you mentioned?

He somehow succeeded in keeping the question confined inside his skull. Because he already knew he wouldn't get an answer. Not until she was good and ready to tell him—if she ever was.

The woman was hiding something. But he had no idea what it was.

The last thing he wanted to do, though, was to fall for her all over again, and then stand around cooling his heels, hoping each time she left that when she returned, she'd be back to stay. He might be a glutton for punishment, but he was no fool.

So what did he do?

For a start, he could act like the scientist he was—examine the evidence without her realizing what he was doing. Just like he found various ways to look at the same specimens in his lab—using dyes, centrifuges, and cultures, until they revealed all their secrets.

He was trained to study things from different angles. His fingers continued to grip hers as he glanced down into those deep green eyes. That's what he had to do. Probe, study, examine—kiss.

Whatever it took.

Until she gave up every last secret. And then he could put his crazy emotions to rest once and for all.

Pure heaven.

Tracy sank into the fragrant bubbles, finding the water cool and inviting. Anything warmer would have been unbearable with the sizzling temperatures outside today. She remembered they hadn't even needed a hot-water heater for their showers in Teresina—the water coming from the taps had been plenty warm enough for almost everything.

She sighed and leaned her head back against the rim of the tub. She had no idea how Ben had arranged to have one of the large blue water tanks brought in and set up behind the house, but he had. He'd also had folding screens erected all around it for privacy.

The tanks were normally installed on residential rooftops as a way to increase water pressure. She'd never heard of bathing in one, but as it was the size of a normal hot tub, it was the perfect depth, really. He'd even managed to rustle up some scented shampoo that had probably come from the local market—although the store hadn't been open since the outbreak had begun.

She hadn't dared strip completely naked, but even clad in her black bra and panties the experience still felt unbelievably decadent. Better yet, Ben had stationed himself outside the screened-off area, making sure no one came upon her unexpectedly—not that they could see much through the thick layer of bubbles.

Why had he done it? Yes, they'd both been exhausted and, yes, despite her tepid showers, her muscles ached with fatigue from turning patients and making sure she moved their arms and legs in an effort to keep blood clots from forming.

Where had he even gotten the tank? It looked new, not like it had been drained and taken off someone's house. Well, once she was done, she'd let him have a turn. Only the bubbles would be gone by then and he'd be getting used water—unless they took the time to refill the thing. And she knew Ben was concerned enough about the environment that he wouldn't want to double their water usage.

Or… She pushed up out of the water and stared down at her chest. Her bra was solid black, so nothing showed through. In fact, her underwear was less revealing than what you'd find on most Brazilian beaches. So maybe he could just join her.

A faint danger signal went off in her head, its low buzz making her blink as she sank back into the water.

What? She wasn't naked. Far from it.

Ben had already seen her with a lot fewer clothes. And it wasn't like anyone was going to venture behind the house. The property itself was walled off with an eight-foot-high concrete fence—which was typical in Brazil. The screens were merely an added layer of protection.

If *she'd* been hot and sweaty when he'd unveiled his surprise, then he had to be positively baking. Especially as he was now standing guard in the sun just beyond the screens. And the water really did feel amazing.

"Ben?" His name came out a little softer than necessary. She figured if he didn't hear her, she could just pretend she hadn't said anything.

"Yep?"

Okay, so she was either going to have to suck it up and ask him if he wanted to join her or just make up some random question.

"Um…I was wondering if you wanted to— I mean the water isn't going to be as fresh once I get out, so do you want to…?" Her throat squeezed off the last of the words.

Ben's face appeared around the side of one of the screens. "Excuse me?"

"As long as we both have some clothes on, we can share the water." She couldn't stop a sigh as she curled a hand around the rim of the tank and peered over the top. "I know you won't pour a new bath for yourself."

"I'm okay." There was definite tension in his jaw, which should serve as an additional warning, but now he was making her feel guilty on top of everything else. Especially when she spied a rivulet of sweat running down the side of his neck, and he lifted a hand to dash it away.

"Come on. Stop being a martyr. You've earned a break. Besides, it'll help cool you off."

"That, I doubt." The words were so low she wasn't sure she'd heard them correctly but, still, he moved into the space, hands low on his hips.

He was soaked, his face red from the heat.

"Look at your shirt, Ben. You're practically steaming." She wouldn't mention the fact that seeing her husband layered in sweat had always been a huge turn-on. Maybe this *was* a mistake. But there was no way she was going to call back her words now. He'd think she was chicken.

So…should you stand up and cluck now…or wait until later?

He mumbled something under his breath that sounded weirdly like, "You're a scientist. Examine, probe…"

The rest of the sentence faded away to nothing.

"Come on, Ben. You're making me feel guilty."

His lips turned up at the edges. "And are you going to make *me* feel guilty if I refuse?"

"Yes." She realized once she'd answered him that his last phrase could have been taken more than one way. But then again she was hearing all kinds of strange stuff today.

When his hands went to the bottom of his shirt and hauled the thing up and over his head, her breath caught in her throat as glistening pecs and tight abs came into view—accompanied by a familiar narrow trail of hair that was every bit as bewitching as she remembered.

Okay, she had definitely not thought this through. For some reason, in her mind she'd pictured him clothed one second and in the tub the next. But then again, stripping outside the fenced area wouldn't help any, because he would still return *sans* most of his clothes.

His hands went to the button of his khaki cargo pants. "You sure about this?"

She gulped. "As long as you have something underneath that."

His smile widened. "It depends whether you're talking about clothing or something else."

Oh, man. She did remember he'd gone commando from time to time, just to drive her crazy. She'd never known when he'd peeled his jeans off at night what she'd find.

When his zip went down this time, however, she breathed a sigh of relief, followed by a glimmer of disappointment, when dark boxers came into view.

As if reading her thoughts, he said, "No reason to any more."

That little ache in her chest grew larger. He no longer had anyone to play those games with.

As he shoved his slacks the rest of the way down his hips and stepped out of them, she tried to avoid looking at him as she thought about how unfair life was. This was a man who should be in a monogamous, loving relationship. He'd been a great husband. A fantastic lover. And he would have made a terrific father.

"You do have clothes on under those bubbles, right?"

"A little late to be asking that now, don't you think?" She wrinkled her nose and snapped the black strap on her shoulder as evidence. "Of course I do. That invitation wouldn't have gone out otherwise."

His smile this time was a bit tight, but he stepped into the huge tub and slid beneath the water in a single quick motion. Too quick to see if the thought of them in this tank together was affecting him as much as it was her.

Oh, lord, she was an idiot. But as the water licked the curve of his biceps with the slightest movement of their bodies, she couldn't bring herself to be sorry she'd given the invitation.

"Nice?" she asked, making sure her bra-covered breasts were well below the waterline. Since it was almost up to her neck, they were nowhere to be seen.

He responded by sinking down further until his head ducked beneath the surface then rose again. A stream of bubble-laden water sluiced down his face, his neck…that strong chest of his… She only realized her eyes were tracking its progress when his voice drew her attention back up.

"Wish I'd thought of doing this days ago."

"Huh?"

He shook his head with a smile. "Nothing. Yeah. It's nice." He stretched his arms out along either side of the tub and watched her. "So, how was your day?"

Maybe this wasn't going to be so weird after all. "Tiring. Yours?"

"Interesting."

"Did General Gutierrez call another meeting?" If Ben had left her out of the loop again, she was going to be seriously miffed. Those were her patients as well. And she'd been first on the scene when the distress call had gone out.

"No, still the same game plan in place, from what I understand." He lowered his hands into the tub and cupped them, carrying the water to his face and splashing it. If he'd been trying to rinse away the remaining bubbles he'd failed because now they'd gathered like a thin goatee on his chin.

"Um…" She motioned to her own chin to let him know.

He scrubbed the offending body part with his shoulder, transferring the bubbles, then took up his position again, arms spread along the curved blue rim. She tried to make herself as small as possible.

"So, you said your day has been interesting. How so?" She kept her hands braced on the bottom of the tub to keep from slipping even further down into the water. Besides, the less of herself she exposed, the less…well, *exposed* she felt.

He shrugged. "Just doing some research."

"On our cases?"

"Our cases. That's exactly it."

She narrowed her eyes. Why did she get the feeling that the word "cases" was being thrown around rather loosely—at least on his side.

"Did you come to any conclusions?"

"Not yet. But I'm hoping to soon."

The look in his eyes was intense, as if he was expecting to see something reflected back at him.

She cleared her throat. "Daniel is almost better. A few

more days and he should be able to be released. Cleo is still complaining of a slight headache, though, and she isn't progressing as quickly as she was earlier."

"Hmm...I'll check her when I get back." His lips pursed. "I've been thinking about those two—Daniel and his sister, I mean. You're good with them."

Something in her stomach tightened. "Like I said earlier, I try to care for all my patients."

"I know you do."

"I feel terrible that their mother didn't..." The tightening spread to her throat, choking off the rest of her words.

"I know, Trace. I'm sorry." He shifted and one of his legs touched hers, his foot lying alongside her knee. She got the feeling the gesture was meant to comfort her because she was too far away for him to reach any other way. The tub was narrower at the bottom than it was at the top, and even though she knew why he'd done it, it still jolted her system to feel the heat of his skin against hers. She returned the pressure, though, to acknowledge what he'd done.

"Thanks," she said. "That means a lot to me."

She licked her lips, expecting him to move his leg away as soon as she said the words, but he didn't. Instead his gaze held hers. What he was expecting her to do, she wasn't quite sure. A shiver went over her when his foot slid along the side of her calf, as if he'd bent his knee beneath the water. Had he done that on purpose?

There was nothing in his expression to indicate he had.

Not only did he not move away, a second later she felt something slide against her other leg. She gulped. Now, that hadn't been an accident. Had it?

And the bubbles were starting to dissipate, popping at an alarming rate. Soon she'd be able to see beneath the water's surface. And so would Ben. So she either needed to wash her hair and get out fast or she needed to stay in and...

That was the question. Just how brave was she?

And exactly how far was she willing to let him go?

CHAPTER TEN

SHE DIDN'T KNOW what to do.

Ben watched the quicksilver shift of expressions cross her face the second his other leg touched hers—puzzlement, realization, concern and finally uncertainty.

"Tracy." He leaned forward and held out his hand to her, keeping his voice low and coaxing. "I know it hasn't been easy coming here—working with me. And I wasn't even sure I wanted you here. But it was the right thing to do."

The right thing to do.

And what about what he was doing now?

He had no idea if it was the right thing or not. But the second she'd invited him into the tub he'd wondered if this was where she'd been heading the whole time. Especially when he'd started shucking his clothes and he'd seen the slightest glimmer of hunger flash through her eyes. She'd quickly doused it, but not before it had registered for what it was. He'd seen that look many a time back when they'd been a couple.

The question was, should he push the boundaries? She was vulnerable. Tired—she'd admitted it herself. Wasn't he taking advantage of that?

He started to pull his hand back when she startled him by reaching out and placing hers within it, saying, "I know it was. So is this."

Without a word she held on tight and tugged, a movement that sent her sliding across the tub towards him. Her feet went up and over his thighs, hitting the curved plastic on either side of his hips. Her forward momentum came to a halt, and his libido took up where momentum left off.

Raw need raced through his system, replacing any ethical questions he'd had a few seconds ago. With a single gesture she'd admitted she wanted him. At least, he hoped that's what it meant.

"When do you need to be back to work?" he asked.

"I'm off until tomorrow." Still two feet away from each other, her gaze swept down his face, lingering on his mouth.

Until tomorrow. That meant he had all night. He forced himself to take a long, slow breath.

He smiled. "You know, we should have thought of putting a tub like this in our back yard. It's almost as big as a pool. The only problem with it is you're still much too far away."

"Am I?" Her thumb swept across the back of his hand beneath the water. "I've come halfway. Maybe it's your turn now."

"Maybe it is." He pushed himself across the space until, instead of being separated by feet, they were now inches apart. "Better?"

She smiled. "Yes, definitely." She released his hand and propped her fingers on his shoulders, smoothing across them and sending fire licking through his gut in the process.

He curled his legs around her backside and reeled her in the rest of the way, until they were breast to chest and she had to tip her head back to look at him.

"So, here we are," he murmured. "What do we do now?"

"Do you have to ask?"

His lips curved in a slow smile. "No, but I thought I should check to make sure we were on the same page."

"Same page of the very same book."

That was all the confirmation he needed. He cupped the back of her head and stared into her eyes before doing as she'd asked: meeting her halfway. More than halfway.

He swore, even as he kissed her, that he was still working on his plan. Still analyzing every piece of information. But that lasted all of two seconds before his baser instincts kicked in and robbed him of any type of higher brain function. He'd hoped to get an inkling of whether or not the old attractions were still there.

They were.

And at the moment that attraction was groveling and begging him not to screw this up by thinking too hard.

So he didn't. The fingers in her hair tightened, the silky strands growing taut between them. A tiny sound exited her throat that Ben definitely recognized. Tracy had always been turned on by control.

His over her. Or at least that's what she let herself believe.

In reality, though, she'd always wanted to control every aspect of her life, whereas he was happy to take things as they came. But in the bedroom it was a different story. Handing him the reins got her motor running, and right now Ben was more than happy to oblige.

Using his grip on her hair to hold her in place, he kissed along one of her gorgeous cheekbones, taking his time as he headed towards her ear.

"Ben."

His eyes closed at the sound of his name on her lips. Oh, yeah. It had been four long years since he'd heard that husky whisper—half plea, half groan. And it drove him just as crazy today as it had back then.

His teeth closed over her earlobe, while his free hand

trailed slowly down the curve of her neck, continuing down her spine in long feathery strokes, until the line of her bra interrupted him. He circled the clasp a time or two, his finger gliding over the lacy strap that transected her back. One snap and he had it undone.

A whimper escaped her throat, but she couldn't move, still held fast by his hand in her hair. He tugged her head back a bit further, exposing the line of her throat, and the vein beating madly beneath her ear. He licked it, pressed his tongue tight against that throbbing pulse point, glorying in the way those rhythmic waves traveled straight to his groin, making him harder than he ever remembered being. Unable to contain his need, he whispered, "I want you. Right here. Right now. Say yes."

She moistened her lips, but didn't keep him waiting long before responding. "Yes."

"Yes." He breathed in the word and released her hair, his hands going to the straps on her shoulders, peeling them down her arms and letting the piece of clothing sink to the bottom of the tank. He parted the bubbles on the surface of the water until her breasts came into full view.

"Beautiful." He cupped them. "Get up on your knees, honey."

She did as he asked, a water droplet clinging to the hard tip of her left nipple. Who could blame it? Certainly not him, because that was right where he wanted to be.

Lowering his head, he licked the drop off, her quick intake of breath telling him she liked the way he lingered, her fingers on the back of his head emphasizing her point.

He pulled away slightly, and looked up at her with hooded eyes. "Ask for it, Tracy."

Her lips parted, but she didn't utter a word, already knowing that wasn't what he was looking for. Instead, she kept her hands braced against his nape, and arched her back until the breast he'd been courting was back against his mouth. She slowly drew the erect nipple along his lower lip.

"That's it," he whispered against her skin. "I love it when you do that."

He opened his mouth, and she shifted closer. When his lips closed around her and sucked, her body went rigid, and she cried out softly. He gave her what she wanted, using his teeth, his tongue to give her the same pleasure she'd just given him. God, he loved knowing what she wanted and making her reach for it. His arms went around her back, his hands sliding beneath the band of her panties and cupping her butt. He slipped his fingers lower and encountered a slick moisture that had nothing to do with the water all around them. Raw need roared through him.

Knowing he was coming close to the edge of his own limits, he found her center and slid a finger deep inside her, then another, reveling in the way she lowered herself until they were fully embedded. He held her steady with one hand while his mouth and fingers swept her along remembered paths, her breathing picking up in time with his movements.

Not long now.

And he was ready for her. More than ready. He ached to be where his fingers were.

He clamped down with his teeth and at the same time applied steady pressure in the depths of her body, and just like in days past, she moaned loudly, her body stiffening as she trembled on the precipice before exploding around his fingers in a series of spasms that rocked his world. Within seconds he'd freed himself and lifted her onto his erection, sweeping aside the crotch of her panties as he thrust hard and deep.

Hell. His breath left his lungs as memories flooded back. Except everything was even better than he remembered, her still pulsing body exquisitely tight, her head thrown back, dark, glossy hair tumbling free around her bare shoulders as she rode him. Over and over, squeezing and releasing, until he could hold back no longer and with a sharp groan he joined her, falling right over the edge into paradise.

CHAPTER ELEVEN

A DISASTER. THAT'S what yesterday's session in the water tank had been.

Tracy stood in front of the tiny mirror in the bathroom and examined her bare breasts. Really looked at them for the first time in a long time. She'd spent the last several years avoiding everything they represented.

And yet they'd brought her such pleasure yesterday.

It was a paradox. One she'd tried to blank out by pretending they didn't exist. Only Ben had forced an awareness that was as uncomfortable as it was real. How much longer was she going to keep running away?

I'm not!

Tracy continued to stare at her reflection, her lips giving a wry twist. She'd believed those two words once, even as she'd scurried from one place to another. Now…? Well, now she wasn't so sure.

She should tell him. Now that the anger was gone, he should know the truth of what she'd been facing back then.

Why? What good could possibly come of it now that they were no longer together? Did she want him to feel guilty for what he'd done? For touching her there?

No. She wanted him to remember it the same way she did—as a pleasurable interlude that shouldn't be repeated.

She raised her hands and cupped herself, remembering

the way Ben's fingers had done the same—the way he'd brought his mouth slowly down…

Shaking her head, she let her arms fall back to her sides.

As great as their time together had been, retracing her steps and venturing back into an unhappy past was not a wise move. Ben had been miserable with her by the end of their marriage.

But how much of that had been her doing? Had been because of what she'd become? A phantom, too scared to sit in any one spot for too long—who had felt the walls of their house closing in around her any time she'd spent more than a couple of weeks there.

So how could she have let yesterday happen?

She had no idea.

Even though she could freely admit it had been a mistake, could even recite each and every reason it had been the wrong thing to do, she couldn't force herself to be sorry for those stolen moments. She'd always known what she'd felt for Ben was powerful—that she'd never feel the same way about another man—and being with him again had just driven that point home.

Which meant she couldn't let it happen again.

Reaching for her clothes, she hurriedly pulled them on, turning her back to the mirror like she always did and feeling like a fraud. It was one thing to admit her reasons for doing something. It was another thing entirely to change her behavior. Especially when that behavior had served her perfectly well for the past four years.

At least…until now.

By the time she made it to the makeshift hospital, Daniel was sitting in a chair next to his bed, his chin on his chest. His eyes were dry, but his arms were wrapped around his waist as if he was in pain.

She squatted next to him. "Daniel, what's wrong? Does something hurt?"

He shook his head, but didn't move from his slumped position.

"Then what is it?"

Several seconds went by before he answered her. "Where will we go?"

The question was so soft she had to lean forward to hear it, and even then she wasn't sure she'd caught his words.

"I'm sorry?"

Lifting his head, he glanced around the space. She twisted to do the same and noted several of the beds were newly empty—fresh sheets neatly pulled up and tucked in as if ready for new patients. Only there probably wouldn't be any.

There'd been no deaths in the last day or so, and the people who'd become ill after the teams had arrived had ended up with much less severe versions of the illness. It definitely made a case for early intervention.

"This is…was our living room…before my mom— before she…" He stopped and took a deep breath. "Once Cleo and I are well enough to leave here, where will we stay?"

Tracy's heart broke all over again. She'd been worrying over her little tryst with Ben when Daniel and Cleo were now facing life without the only parent they'd ever known. And because the two had no relatives that anyone knew of, and as their home was now being used as a temporary hospital, there was literally nowhere for the siblings to go once they were cleared of infection. Oh, the military would probably take them to a state-run orphanage once the quarantine period was lifted. But until then? No one was allowed in or out of the village.

Surely they could stay here in what had once been their home. But where? Every room was being used, whether to house soldiers or medical personnel. It was full. More than full. Even Pedro—whom she'd barely had a chance to speak to in recent days—had moved from where he'd been staying and was now bunking with members of the military unit assigned to São João dos Rios.

She thought for a minute. Ben kept talking about how much he cared about these kids. Maybe it was time to put that to the test. "We can ask to have two more hammocks put up in the room where Dr. Almeida and I sleep. At least until we figure something else out."

Once she'd said it she wondered if that wouldn't make the whole thing feel a little too much like a family for comfort. And she didn't want to give Daniel and Cleo the idea that they could stay together permanently. Because that wasn't on the cards.

Besides, she wasn't sure Ben would be thrilled about sharing his room with a preteen and a child, especially after the slow smile he'd given her that morning. The one that had her face heating despite her best efforts. He'd even stayed and slept in his own hammock last night—a first since they'd arrived. Was it because of what they'd done?

She must have thought so because it was what had set off the self-examination in the bathroom. She hadn't touched herself like that in a long time.

"Will the soldiers let us go with you?" Daniel gave her a hopeful smile.

No backing out now.

"I don't see why they wouldn't, but you'll have to get well first, which means you'll need to get some rest." What else could she say? They couldn't just let Daniel and Cleo wander the streets or sleep in one of the unoccupied houses. The pair had had a home and a family not three weeks ago. And now it was all gone.

She'd been there, done that. She could at least try to help these children as much as she could before she had to leave—be their temporary family, kind of like a foster-care situation. At least until they figured out something a little more permanent.

How was she supposed to do that before she headed back to São Paulo?

Something she didn't want to think about right now.

Just then, Ben walked into the room, his brow raised in question when he saw the two of them sitting together. She stood, glancing down at Daniel, and noted with horror he had a huge smile on his face.

Don't, Daniel. Not yet. Let me talk to him first.

But even as she thought it, the boy spoke up. "Tracy says Cleo and I can stay with you once we are well."

Ben's glance shot to her. "She did? When?"

"Just now. I explained we did not have any place to go, and she offered to let us stay with you. Cleo was scared." He blinked a couple of times as if that last statement had been hard for him to admit. "We both were…about what might happen. If they tried to take Cleo away from me…" He didn't finish the rest of his statement.

Ben's face grew stormy. "Tracy? Would you like to explain?"

"I, um… Well, I simply said we would figure something out…"

"Figure something out," he parroted.

Daniel's smile never wavered. He had no idea Ben's now icy glare was sucking the heat right out of the atmosphere.

Nodding, Daniel continued, "Yes, so Cleo and I wouldn't be alone—so we could stay together."

Oh, no! He'd obviously misunderstood her intentions—had thought she'd meant the living arrangements would continue even after they left the town. Ben was going to blow his top.

"Well, Daniel, I'm glad to hear she's making those kinds of plans." He moved toward her. "Can I borrow her for a minute?"

"Yes, I have to tell Cleo the good news, anyway. One of the doctors is helping her walk around the yard outside. She should be back in a minute."

Right on cue, Cleo and her companion came through the door and made their way slowly towards them.

"Tracy, do you mind?" Giving a sharp nod toward the door to indicate she should follow him, Ben stalked toward it.

Gulping back her own dismay, she forced a smile to her face. "I won't be long. Could you tell Cleo I'll be back to check on you both in a few minutes?"

As upset as Ben was, she couldn't help but feel a fierce sense of gratitude over the kids' steady improvement. From all indications, they were going to recover fully.

Two miracles in a sea of sorrows.

They'd lost fourteen patients in all. In such a tiny village it was a good percentage of the population. They'd have a hard time coming back from this without some type of government aid. Whether that meant sending them to another town and bulldozing these homes, or finding a way to get things up and running again, nothing would truly be the same again. They would not soon forget what had happened here.

Neither would she.

Pushing through the door, she saw that Ben was already striding down the hallway on his way out of the house. She hurried after him, knowing he must be furious. But once he heard her explanation, he'd understand that...

The second the bright noonday sun hit her retinas, a hand reached out and tugged her to the side, into the shadow of the house.

"Would you like to tell me what the hell that was all about? You expect those kids to stay with us once we leave here? Kind of hard, as we no longer live in the same house. Or even the same state."

"No. Of course not. He took my words the wrong way. I was only talking about here in the village. That they could stay in our room once they left the hospital." She reached out to squeeze his fingers then let go. "They have nowhere else to go. I didn't know what to say."

"So you said they could stay with us?" He swore softly. "Are you that worried about being alone with me, Tracy?"

She looked at him blankly for a second or two. "What are you talking about?"

"I'm talking about what happened between us yesterday." He propped his hands on his hips. "I think it's a little late to start worrying about your virtue—or reputation—or whatever you want to call it."

What a ridiculous thing for him to say. "You're wrong. This has nothing to do with what happened. Nothing."

"Then why?"

Was it her imagination, or was there a shadow of hurt behind his pale eyes?

"They have nowhere to go until the outbreak is over. This was their house, remember? Once they're released from care, they'll be expected to leave, just like our other patients have. They have no relatives here—or anywhere else, if what Daniel said was true."

Ben pivoted and leaned against the wall, dragging a hand through his hair, which was already damp from the heat of the day. "You're right. I thought…"

Since he didn't finish his sentence, she had no idea *what* he thought.

Maybe he was worried she was making a play for him. That she wanted to move back to their old house. No, that didn't make any sense. He'd given no hint he wanted to start things back up between them. For all she knew, he'd just needed to get laid, and she'd practically put up a neon sign saying she was ready, willing and able to take care of that need.

What had she been thinking, inviting him to get in the tub?

Well, it was over and done with. They were both adults. They *both* had needs—heaven knew, hers hadn't been met in quite some time. Four years, to be exact. She hadn't been with anyone since she'd left him.

To say that the experience yesterday had been cataclysmic was an understatement. A huge one.

"Maybe we can put up a curtain or something." She pressed her shoulder to the wall and looked up at him. "Can they stay with us? At least for a little while?"

"Of course they can." The words were soft, but he seemed distracted, almost as if his mind was already on something else entirely. "I'll check with General Gutierrez, and see what he can do about finding them a place to stay after the quarantine is lifted."

"Thank you." She leaned closer and stretched up to kiss his cheek, her hand going to his arm and lingering there. "And I'm sorry Daniel dropped it on you like that. He asked, and it was the only thing I could think of. I was hoping to talk to you alone before we made any decisions."

"What are you going to do about the other part? If he misunderstood, someone is going to have to talk to him."

"I know." She blew out a breath. "Let's give it a few days, though, okay? Until they're stronger and we see how things are going to play out here. Maybe someone in the town can take them in."

"That might pose a bit of a problem." He paused before covering her hand with his own. "I came by to tell you something is getting ready to happen."

Her internal radar went on high alert. "With the military?"

"Yes. I sat in on another meeting today." His jaw tightened. "The news wasn't good. And despite what you think, my opinion doesn't always hold that much sway."

Her skin grew clammy at the way he said it. "What are they going to do?"

Tracy had heard tell of things going on behind the scenes where the military police were concerned. Although many were honest, hard-working, family men, there were others who wouldn't think twice about asking for a bribe.

She'd also heard stories about other branches of the police colluding with the drug cartels that worked out of the *favelas*. The shanty towns were notorious for narcotics and illegal dealings. Many of the slums actually had armed thugs guarding the roads leading to the rickety housing developments. It was not only dangerous for the police to enter such places, it was often deadly. Only the corrupt cops could enter and leave with impunity.

"Nothing's been decided for sure. They're still discussing options with the central government."

The hair on the back of her neck rose at the quiet way he said it. She thought again about Daniel's words and the way she'd found him sitting in that chair. He'd seemed almost hopeless. An unsettling thought occurred to her.

"When Daniel mentioned having nowhere to go, I assumed he was talking about for the next several days. But you and he both jumped to the same conclusion about my offer. You both thought the offer was something more permanent."

"Yes."

"Why is that?" Her voice dropped to a whisper. "What's going to happen here, Ben?"

When she tried to drop her hand from his arm, he held on, fingers tightening around hers. "Remember I told you they were going to lift the quarantine in another week? That we—along with the rest of the medical and military personnel—would be allowed to leave once there were no new cases of the plague?"

"I remember."

"Have you looked around you lately? At the survivors?"

She tried to think. One young mother said her husband was trying to pack all their belongings. She'd assumed it was because they wanted to leave for a while to try to forget the horrors of what had happened here. But what if that was not the reason at all? "I know one couple is preparing to leave. So the military must be planning on lifting the quarantine for everyone at the same time."

"Oh they're lifting it all right. The people you mentioned aren't the only ones getting ready for a big move. There are signs of packing going on all over town. Windows being boarded up. *Acerolas* being bulk-harvested from trees."

She had noticed the berries being picked and put into baskets.

"So everyone is going to leave when this is over? They're going to board up the entire town?" If so, what did that mean for Daniel and Cleo?

"No, they're not going to board it up."

"What, then?"

He drew a deep breath then released it on a sigh. "They're planning to destroy the town once this is all over."

Her eyes widened. "Destroy it? How?"

"The same way they're destroying the bodies. They're going to torch everything, until nothing is left of this place but ashes."

CHAPTER TWELVE

A FAMILY. HE'D always wanted one, but not this way. Not at someone else's expense. And certainly not at the expense of an entire village.

He could still hear the pained cry Tracy had given when he'd told her the news.

Ben leaned against the wall as she helped Daniel attach one end of the hammock to the protective iron grating that covered the window. She gave the rope a tug to make sure it would hold. He'd offered to help, only to have her wave him off, saying Daniel needed something to do.

Maybe she did as well.

He tried to read her body language and the furtive glances she periodically threw his way. They hadn't had much of a chance to talk since she'd had to go back to work at the hospital, but her horror when he'd shared the military's plans had been obvious. They both knew it happened in various countries. Not just in Brazil. It could even happen in the United States, if there were ever a deadly enough epidemic. The same heartbreaking choice might have to be made: contain it, for the good of the general population.

In this case, he wasn't sure it *was* the only option. But in a poor state like *Piauí*, it was the easiest one. São João dos Rios was pretty far off the beaten path. It would be expensive for the military to come in and check the village periodically to make sure the outbreak didn't erupt again, as they still hadn't isolated the initial source of the infection. And if it did recur and spread to a place like *Teresina*—the state capital—it could affect hundreds of thousands of people. If he thought fourteen deaths were far too many, how would he feel if that number was multiplied tenfold?

Hopefully Tracy realized he'd been upset for another reason entirely when she'd explained about Daniel and Cleo sharing their room. And the spark that had lit in his gut when Daniel had talked about them all living together had been hard to contain once it had started burning, although he'd better find a way to extinguish it quickly, because Tracy had no intention of letting this arrangement become permanent.

Well, neither did he.

But he *had* been hoping to have Tracy to himself a little while longer before they went their separate ways. Why he wanted that, he wasn't sure. Maybe just to understand her reasons for inviting him into that tub. To say it had been unexpected would be an understatement.

That was the least of his worries right now, however. The folks in charge were concerned about this getting out to the press. Yeah, hearing that your own military had sluiced cans of gasoline over an entire village and set it ablaze would not be the most popular story. Which was why they were trying to go about it quietly and peacefully. They'd spread the word that stipends would be awarded to anyone who agreed to leave town after the quarantine was lifted.

If they could relocate all the townsfolk before the match was struck, no one would be the wiser—except Ben and a few other key people—until long after the fact. Telling Tracy had probably been a mistake, in fact. But given their history—and her distrust of the military—what else could he have done? Keeping this to himself would have given her one more reason to hate him.

As far as Ben was concerned, as long as no one was hurt, these were just buildings. But he knew Tracy would feel differently. It was one point they'd argued about in the past. He tended to see things with a scientific bent, rather than an emotional one. But it was also one of the things he'd loved about her. She was the balance to his cold, analytical stance, forcing him to see another side to issues. Which made his actions in the past seem childish and petty. If he'd waited until she'd gotten home to talk to her calmly and explained his concerns, would things have turned out differently?

Possibly. There was no way to know.

But it was another of the reasons he'd talked about the military's plans this time. Nothing good could come from discovering the truth from someone else. If she realized he'd kept the information to himself, she'd be furious. And that's the last thing he wanted. Especially after their time in that home-made hot tub—or cooling tub, in this case.

Daniel secured the last of the knots and tried to hop onto the hammock to check it out, but ended up being flipped back onto the floor instead. He lay there panting as if he was exhausted, which he probably was. He was still weak from his illness. Ben pushed away from the wall and reached the boy before Tracy did, holding out a hand. "Easy. You need to regain some strength before trying stuff like that. Besides, you've been on a cot for the last week and a half. You'll have to get used to sleeping in a hammock again."

Daniel let Ben help him up and then rubbed his backside with a rueful grin. "I feel so much better than before, so I forget." He glanced around the space, already cramped from three hammocks. "Where will Cleo sleep?"

"We'll string another hammock above yours. Kind of

like bunk beds. Only you're taller, so you'll sleep in the top one." Ben nodded at the bars on the windows. "They're strong enough to support both hammocks."

Tracy stood next to him. "Good idea. I was beginning to wonder how we were all going to fit."

He gave her a pained smile. "I could always put you up on top, but…" He let the words trail off, knowing she'd catch his implication.

True to form, pink stained both her cheeks, and she turned away to adjust the fan they'd brought in from one of the other rooms. "This will help keep the mosquitoes away, as most of nets are being used by the hospital."

"We never used them at home anyway," Daniel said.

Tracy's sister had died of dengue fever, so she was a little more paranoid about using the netting than many Brazilians. He couldn't blame her. He still remembered the day he'd come home to find the milky netting draped across their huge canopy bed. Despite the fact that her reasons for putting it up had had nothing to do with romance and everything to do with safety, he still found it incredibly intimate once they were both inside. And when he'd made love to her within the confines of the bed, there'd been a raw, primitive quality to Tracy that had shaken him to the core. She'd fallen pregnant that night.

A shaft of pain went through him.

Her eyes met his and she gave a rueful smile, her face growing even pinker. She was remembering those nights as well. He could at least be glad some of those memories made her smile, rather than filling her with bitterness.

And then there were these two kids. What was going to happen to them if the village really was burned down?

Something else he was better off not thinking about, because there wasn't a thing he could do about it.

Tracy says Cleo and I can stay with you once we are well.

If only it were that easy.

Wasn't it?

He swallowed, the words replaying in his head again and again. Evidently that "bath" had permanently messed something up in his skull. Was he actually thinking about taking on somebody else's kids?

He forced his mind back to the mosquito-net conversation between Tracy and Daniel, which was still going strong.

Interrupting her, he said, "We haven't been using nets either, Trace. It's not dengue season anyway."

"I know."

He sensed she wanted to say something further, maybe even about their current situation, but Daniel's presence made sharing any kind of confidences more complicated, if not impossible. And that went for any other kind of intimacies they might have shared in this room. Because with Daniel officially sprung from the infirmary, there was no possibility of that. But he would have liked to have talked to Tracy about…stuff.

Maybe even apologize for his actions four years ago.

"Will they still let me see Cleo?"

Surprisingly, Daniel had recovered faster than his sister, who would be in the infirmary for another day or so. And if he knew Tracy, she'd be sleeping in a chair next to the girl's bed, in case Daniel's absence made her jittery.

Tracy glanced at her watch. "I don't see why not. It's only seven o'clock. Curfew isn't for another three hours."

That was another thing. Yesterday, the military had suddenly instituted a curfew without warning. They'd said it was to prevent looting now that more people were recovering, but Ben had a feeling it had more to do with news being passed from person to person than anything else. Why prevent looting in a place they were planning to burn down?

No, it made no sense, other than the fact it was easier to keep an eye on folks during the daytime. If they imposed a curfew, they had more control over what went on after dark.

"Okay," Daniel said, then hesitated. "Do you need me to help with anything else?"

Tracy shook her head and smiled at him. "No, just be back by ten—tell Cleo I'll be there in a little while. And we'll try to rustle up a snack before bedtime, okay? We need to build up your strength."

The concern in her voice made Ben's heart ache. Tracy would have been a good mother had her job not consumed her every waking moment.

Job or no job, though, his own behavior back then wasn't something he was proud of.

It made him even more determined to set the record straight and see if they could make peace about the past. With Daniel sharing their room, he wasn't sure when he'd get the chance. But he intended to try. The sooner the better.

Tracy glanced at the door as it closed behind Daniel. She was still having trouble processing what Ben had told her. They were going to burn the town down? Without letting anyone have a say?

What would happen to Daniel and Cleo if that happened? She'd hoped maybe someone here would be willing to take on the kids since places like São João dos Rios tended to be close-knit communities. But if they all were forced to scatter in different directions, the kids might end up in a slum or an orphanage...or worse.

"What are those kids going to do now, Ben?" She pulled her hair up into a loose ponytail and used the elastic she wore around her wrist to secure it in place. Her neck felt moist and sticky, despite the gusts of warm air the fan pushed their way from time to time.

"I don't know." He leaned down to the tiny refrigerator he'd brought from his lab and opened the door. Tossing her a cold bottle of water, he took one out for himself, twisting the top and taking a long pull.

Tracy paused to press her bottle against her overheated face, welcoming the shock of cold as it hit her skin. Closing her eyes, she rolled the plastic container along her cheek until she reached her hairline, before repeating the action on the other side. Then she uncapped the bottle and sipped at it. "There's something to be said about cold water. Thanks."

"No problem. How long do you think he'll be?"

"Daniel?" She turned to look at him, suspicion flaring within her. "He'll probably be a while. He and Cleo are close."

"They certainly seem to be."

Surely he wasn't thinking about trying something in the boy's absence. "Why did you ask?"

"What Daniel said made me think about their future, and I thought we could try to figure something out, especially if the military's plans become a reality."

"What can we do?"

"I'm not sure." He scrubbed a hand across the back of his neck. "Maybe one of the villagers could take the kids with them when they leave."

"I thought about that as well, but I don't see how. The whole town will be uprooted and scattered. Most of them will have to live with other people for a while, until they get back on their feet. Adding two more mouths to the equation…?" She took a quick drink.

"You know how these things work, Ben. The people here are barely scraping by. To lose their homes, their livelihood? The last thing they'll be thinking about is two orphaned kids—no matter how well liked they are."

And how was she going to walk away from them when the time came? How could she bear to look those children in the eye with an apologetic shrug and then climb into Ben's car?

There was a long pause. Then Ben said in a low voice, "Ever since Daniel misunderstood what you meant, something's been rattling around in my head."

"Really? What?"

Before he could say anything, Daniel came skidding down the hallway, his face as white as the wall behind him. "Please, come. Cleo is sick. Really sick."

CHAPTER THIRTEEN

Tracy stroked Cleo's head, while Ben glanced at the read-out. "Almost three hundred. No wonder she's not feeling well."

Her blood-sugar levels were sky-high.

"She's mentioned having a headache on and off, but I thought it was because of the plague. I had no idea. Is she diabetic?"

"I don't know." He glanced at Pedro, who was standing near the head of the bed and had been the one to send Daniel to find them. "Did anyone notice her breath smelling off?"

A fruity smell was one sign of diabetes, and something one of them should have noticed.

Tracy bristled at his tone, however. "We've been fighting the plague for the last week and a half, Ben. We weren't looking for anything else."

"It wasn't a criticism. Just a question. Would you mind calling Daniel back into the room?"

Poor Daniel. He'd been banished as they'd tried to assess a thrashing Cleo, who not only had a headache but stomach cramps as well. It had seemed to take ages for Ben to get the finger-prick. They'd need to get a urine sample as well to make sure the child's body wasn't flooded with ketones. Without enough insulin to break down sugar, the body would begin converting fat into energy. That process resulted in ketones, which could quickly grow to toxic levels.

Cleo had quieted somewhat, but she was still restless on her cot, her head twisting back and forth on the pillow.

The second the boy came into the room, Ben asked him, "Does your sister have diabetes?"

"Diabetes?" A blank stare was all he received. "Is it from this sickness we had?"

Of course he wouldn't know anything about glucose levels or what too much sugar circulating in the bloodstream could lead to. Many of these people didn't get regular medical care. And what they did get was confined to emergencies or critical illnesses. Surely if the girl had type-one diabetes, though, someone would have figured it out. "Could her glucose levels have been affected by the plague?" Tracy asked.

"Possibly. Serious illnesses can wreak havoc on some of those balances. Or maybe her pancreas was affected. The plague isn't always confined the lungs. We'll pray the change is temporary, but in the meantime we need to get some insulin into her and monitor her blood-sugar levels."

"And if it's not temporary?"

"Let's take one thing at a time." Ben stripped off his gloves and tossed them, along with the test strip, into the wastebasket. "If the glucose doesn't stabilize on its own, we'll have to transport her somewhere so she can be diagnosed and treated."

"The hospital in *Teresina* is good."

Jotting something in a spiralbound notebook, he didn't even look up. "But she doesn't live in *Teresina*."

"She doesn't live anywhere. Not any more."

Unfortunately, she'd forgotten that Daniel was in the room. He immediately jumped on her statement. "But I thought we were going to live with you."

She threw Ben a panicked glance and was grateful when he stopped writing and came to the rescue.

"We're still hammering out the details."

Oh, Lord, how were they going to fix this? Hoping that one of the villagers would take the kids had already been a long shot. But if Cleo did have diabetes, it was doubtful if anyone from São João dos Rios would have the resources to take on her medical expenses.

She could offer to take the kids herself, but things in her life could change at any moment. Just that morning she'd faced that fact while staring in the mirror. She was going to have to do something about those test results—like sit down with a doctor and discuss her options. The more she thought about it, though, the more she was leaning toward a radical solution, a permanent one that would give her peace of mind once and for all. For the most part, anyway.

Maybe she could talk to Ben. Tell him what she was facing. And ask him if he would take the kids instead, at least on a temporary basis. Just until they figured out what was going on with Cleo.

And if he said no?

Then she had no idea what she was going to do. But one thing was for sure. She was not going to abandon Cleo. Not without doing everything in her power to make sure the girl was in good hands.

After they got a dose of insulin into her, they monitored her for the next two hours, until her blood-sugar levels began to decrease. An hour before curfew and knowing there would be little sleep to be had, Tracy asked Ben to walk with her to get a cup of coffee from the cafeteria, leaving Pedro and Daniel to stand watch. Several carafes were still on the buffet table, left over from the evening meal. Two of the pitchers even had some warm dregs left in them. Ben handed her a cup of the thick, black liquid and she spooned some sugar into hers to cut the bitter edge, while Ben drank his plain.

He made a face. "Not quite like I make at home."

Tracy smiled. "You always did make great coffee."

They wandered over to one of the tables at the back of the room. Ben waited for her to sit then joined her.

She nursed her cup for a moment before saying anything. "Do you think Cleo's blood sugar is going to drop back to normal once she's better?"

"I hope so."

"Ben…about what Daniel said…" She drew a deep breath and then blurted it out. "Maybe you could take them."

"Take them where? They don't have family that we know of."

Oh, boy. Something was about to hit that wheezy fan in the window behind her. But she had to ask. Had to try. "No, I mean maybe you could take them in for a while. Make sure Cleo gets the treatment she needs. It wouldn't have to be permanent."

Ben's brows drew together, and he stared at her for several long seconds. "What?"

Once the words were out, there was no retracting them, and they just seemed to keep tumbling from her mouth. "You always said you wanted kids. Well, this is the perfect solution—you won't even need a wife to birth them for you."

"I won't need a wife to…birth them?" His frown grew even stormier. "Is that how you felt about your pregnancy? That I was dooming you to be some type of brood mare? And our baby was just an inconvenience to be endured?"

"Oh, Ben, of course not. I wanted that baby as much as you did." She set her coffee down and wrapped her hands around the cup. "There were just circumstances that… Well, it doesn't matter now."

"What circumstances?"

"I don't want to talk about that. I want to figure out how to help these kids."

"And your way of doing that is by asking someone else to take them on?" He blew out an exasperated breath. "What are they supposed to do while I'm at work? Cleo can't monitor her own blood sugar."

"Daniel is practically a teen. And he's already displayed an enormous amount of responsibility. If she is diabetic, he could help." She plowed ahead. "You've seen how well behaved they are. They could—"

"I can't believe you're putting this all on me, Tracy." His fingers made angry tracks through his hair. "If you feel so strongly about it, why don't *you* take them?"

She knew it was an illogical thought, but if she ended up having surgery, who would watch the kids while she was recovering? It wasn't simply a matter of removing her breasts and being done with it. She wanted reconstruction afterwards. Each step of the process took time. Hospital time. Recovery time.

Both physical and emotional.

She decided to be honest as much as she could. "I can't take them, Ben. If I thought there was any way, believe me, I'd be the first to step up to the plate. They beat the odds and survived the outbreak—when none of us thought they could—so it just doesn't seem fair to abandon them to the system."

"Said as if it's a jail sentence."

"*Teresina* is poor. I've seen the orphanages, remember? I was one of the physicians who helped care for those children when I lived there."

"Let's go for a walk." He stood, collecting both of their half-empty cups. "I don't want Daniel to come in and find us arguing over his fate."

Fate. What a funny word to use. But it was true. What

Ben decided right here, right now, would determine those kids' futures. He could make sure Cleo got the treatment she needed. Even if this was a temporary setback, getting her glucose levels under control could take time.

Ben tossed the cups in the wastebasket and headed out the door, leaving Tracy to hurry to catch up with him.

"Won't you at least consider it?" she asked, turning sideways as she walked next to one of several abandoned houses.

He blew out a rough breath. "I don't know what you want me to say here, Tracy. I'll have to think about it. It would help to know why you're so dead set against taking them yourself."

"I travel a lot. My career—"

"Don't." The angry throbbing of a vein in his temple showed how touchy a subject this was. "Don't even play the travel card—you already know how I feel about that. Besides, I have a career too. So do millions of parents everywhere. But most of them at least want to spend a little time with their husbands and kids."

Shock roiled through her. Was that how he'd seen her? She'd known he hadn't like her traveling. Known it was because of how his parents had treated him and his brother, but hearing him say it outright hurt on a level it never had before.

"I did want to spend time with you." Her voice was quiet when it came out.

She should have told him the truth, long ago. But when he'd sent the military after her as she'd been trying to figure out how to tell him about the test results, she'd felt hurt and betrayed. And terribly, terribly angry. Angry at him, angry about her mother's death and angry that her future might not be the one she'd envisioned.

Maybe she'd turned a large part of that anger on Ben, somehow rationalizing that he didn't deserve to know the truth after what he'd done to her. Convinced herself that she didn't care what he thought—or that he might view her behavior through the lens of his childhood.

Abandoned by his parents. Abandoned by his wife.

What did that make her?

She closed her eyes, trying to block out the thought of Ben sitting alone at home night after night, while she'd tried to outrun her demons. "It's okay. If you can't take them, I'll find someone else."

"Who?"

"Pedro, maybe."

The frown was back. "You'd really ask your assistant to take two kids that you're not willing to take yourself?"

Her eyes filled with tears. "It's not that I'm not willing to. There are times I think about what our child might have looked like and I… Maybe I can take them for a while and then figure something else out." She bit her lip, unable to control the wobble of her chin.

Ben took a step forward so she was forced to look up at him then brushed wisps of hair from her temples. His hands slid around to cradle the back of her head. "I didn't say I wouldn't take them. I just said I needed to think about it. So give me a day or two, okay?"

She nodded, her heart thumping in her chest as his touch chased away the regret and did strange things to her equilibrium. "Okay."

"How do you do it?" He leaned down and slid his cheek across hers, the familiar coarseness of his stubble wrenching at her heart.

"Do what?"

"Talk me into doing crazy stuff."

"I—I don't."

"No?" His breath swept across her ear, sending a shiver over her. "How about talking me into getting in that tub?"

Oh. He was right. She had been the one who'd invited

him in. "Maybe it's not me. Maybe it's this climate. The heat messes with your brain."

"Oh, no. This is all you. *You* mess with my brain."

She didn't know if he thought she messed with it in a bad way or a good way. She suddenly hoped it was good. That he remembered their life together with some fondness, despite the heartache she'd caused him.

His lips touched her cheek then grazed along it as he continued to murmur softly to her. "Tell you what. The kids can come live at the house—temporarily, until Cleo is better and we can find something else."

She wasn't sure she'd heard him correctly. She pulled away to look at him, although the last thing she wanted was for his mouth to stop what it was doing. "You'll take them?"

"I think you missed the pronoun. I said 'we.'"

"What do you mean?"

"I'm not going to do this by myself. If Cleo's condition doesn't stabilize and this turns into full-blown diabetes, she'll need to be transported back and forth to a specialist. Her insulin levels will need to be monitored closely at first."

"Daniel—"

"Daniel is responsible, yes, but he's still just a kid. He's grieving the loss of his mother. I don't think it's fair to expect him to take on the bulk of Cleo's care."

"I agree."

"So the 'we' part of the equation means we share the load. You and me." His sly smile warned her of what was coming before his words had a chance to register. "Until *we* can arrange something else, you'll need to come back to Teresina. With me."

CHAPTER FOURTEEN

"WHAT?"

Ben had expected an angry outburst the second she realized what he was asking. What he didn't anticipate was the stricken pain that flooded her eyes instead.

Warning bells went off inside him.

"It won't be that hard. You can relocate for six months to a year—help the kids get through one school year. You'll be closer to the Amazon, anyway, if you're in *Teresina*, because *Projeto Vida's* medical boat operates out of *Manaus*."

She stopped walking and turned to face him. "Ben, I—I can't."

Something in her face took him aback. What was going on here?

"Why can't you? And if you mention the word 'travel,' the deal is off." He held his ground. "I want Cleo to get the best treatment available. In fact, I want that just as much as you do, but you've got to tell me why you can't sacrifice one year of your life to help make sure she does."

She turned away from him and crossed over to the trunk of a huge mango tree, fingering the bark.

Not about to let her off the hook, he followed her, putting his hands on her shoulders. She whirled round to face him.

"You want to know why I'm reluctant to commit to a

year in Teresina? Why I traveled so much while I was carrying our child?"

"Yes." He kept his eyes on hers, even as the first tears
spilled over her lashes.

"Because I have the BRCA1 mutation. And I don't know
when—or even if—that switch might suddenly flip on."

"BRCA…" His mind went blank for a second before his
training kicked in. "One of the breast-cancer markers?"

A lot of information hit his system at once: Tracy's
mother's early death from the disease, her grandmother's
death. Next came shock. She'd been tested for the gene
variation? There's no way she'd draw that kind of conclusion without some kind of definitive proof. "When did
you find out?"

"A while ago." Her green eyes skipped away from his.
"After my mother passed away."

An ugly suspicion went through his mind. Her mom had
died not long after they'd married. A lot of things suddenly
became clear. The frantic pace she'd kept. Her withdrawal
a month or so before she'd finally walked out on him. "It
was while you were pregnant, wasn't it?"

She nodded.

"You went through genetic testing and never said a
word to me?"

"I didn't want to worry you. And then when the test
came back positive…" She shook her head. "I was trying
to think of a way to tell you. Before I could, you sent the
military into that village. I was angry. Hurt. And then I
lost the baby."

And then she'd lost the baby.

A streak of raw fury burst through his system closing
off his throat and trapping all kinds of angry words inside as he remembered that time. She'd stood in his office
a week and a half ago and accused him of going behind

her back, and yet she'd traipsed around the country, carrying this huge secret.

Oh, no. That was where he drew the line.

"Yes, I did go behind your back, and I was wrong for doing that. But how is that any different than what you did? You went behind *my* back and had yourself tested for a gene that could impact your life…our future as a couple. How could you have kept that a secret?"

"You're right, Ben. I'm sorry." Her hands went to his, which had drawn up into tight fists as he'd talked. Her fingers curved around them. "At first I was just scared, wondering what it meant for our baby—and if it was a girl, if I would pass the gene to her. Then I worried about how this would affect us as a couple. I—I didn't want your pity."

"Believe me, pity is the last thing I'm feeling right now." At the top of the list was anger. Anger that she'd suffered in silence. Anger that she hadn't trusted him enough to say anything.

"I probably should have told you. I know that now."

"Probably? *Probably?* I cannot believe you just used that word."

She swallowed. "Okay, I *should* have told you."

"We were supposed to be a couple, Tracy. A team. I shared every part of my life with you. Didn't keep one thing from you."

"I know it doesn't seem right. But when you've had some time to think about it—"

"I don't need time to think."

When he started to pull away from her completely, she gripped his wrists, holding him in place. "Try to understand, Ben. My mom had died of cancer six months after we were married. We got pregnant sooner than we expected to, and I started to worry. Being tested was something I did on impulse, just to put my mind at ease. I didn't expect the results to come back the way they did."

"And yet you kept them to yourself. Even when they did."

"Yes."

The anger drained out of him, leaving him exhausted. "It explains everything."

And yet it explained nothing.

Not really. Millions of women faced these same kinds of decisions. And most of them didn't shut their loved ones out completely. Only Tracy had also been facing the loss of their child in addition to the test results. Not to mention what she'd viewed as a betrayal on his part.

He wrapped his arms around her and pulled her close, tucking her head against his shoulder.

"I'm sorry, Ben," she repeated. The low words were muffled by his shirt, but he heard them, sensed they were coming from her heart.

He didn't respond, just let the charged emotions crash over him until they were all spent.

Nothing could change what had happened back then. It was what it was. She'd made her decision, and now he had to make his. How he was going to handle this new-found knowledge?

"This is why you don't want to take Daniel and Cleo yourself."

"Yes."

Wow. He tried to find the right words but found himself at a loss. Maybe like she'd been when she'd found out?

He gripped her upper arms and edged her back a little so he could look at her face. Fresh tear tracks had appeared, although she hadn't let out any kind of sound.

"This isn't a death sentence, Tracy." He wiped the moisture from her cheeks and eyes with the pad of his thumb. "Carrying the gene mutation doesn't mean you'll develop the disease."

"My mom and grandmother did."

"I know. But knowledge is power. You know to be vigilant."

"I know that I might have to take preventative measures."

Something she'd hinted at earlier. "Tamoxifen?" He'd heard that some of the chemo drugs were being used as a preventative measure nowadays, much like the antibiotics they'd used on those exposed to the plague in São João dos Rios. All in the hope of killing any cancer cells before they had a chance to develop and multiply.

"Some women choose to go that route, yes."

"But not you." It was a statement, because from her phrasing it was clear that she wasn't looking at that option. Or had looked at it and rejected it.

"No. Not me." She licked her lips. "I've been weighing the benefits of prophylactic surgery."

"Surgery..." He blinked as he realized exactly what she was saying. "You're thinking of having an elective mastectomy?" Against his will, his glance went to her chest and then back to her face.

"Yes. That's what I'm saying. I don't know the timing yet, but I realized not long ago that if I can head it off, that's what I'm going to do."

Shit.

He remembered their time in the tub and how he'd gently caressed her breasts. Kissed them. What had she been thinking as he'd brought her nipples to hard peaks? Even then, she hadn't said a word. Maybe she had been committing the sensations to memory.

Okay, now *his* vision was starting to go a little funny. He tightened his jaw. Tracy had said the last thing she wanted from him was pity. He needed to suck it up. Then again, she'd had a whole lot longer to process the information than he had. And ultimately she was right. It was her decision to make. He might disagree or object or even urge her to go ahead and do it, but he wasn't the one who'd have to live with the aftermath. Tracy was.

And he'd had no idea what she'd been facing all this time. He was surprised she hadn't chosen to have the surgery right after their break-up.

He decided not to say anything. Instead, he opted to go a completely different route.

But before he could, she spoke again. "So you see why I'm reluctant to say yes. I was planning to meet with a doctor when I got back to São Paulo."

"Give it some time, Tracy. Neither one of us should make any hard and fast decisions right on the heels of fighting this outbreak." He tucked a lock of hair behind one of her ears. "I'll be honest, though. I don't think I can commit to taking on Cleo's treatment on my own. And I'm not sure it would be fair to her or Daniel. I'm away a lot. Sometimes for days at a time."

"Kind of like I used to be." The words had a ring of challenge to them.

"The difference is I don't have a partner or children at home. Not any more."

She sighed. "And I did."

His thumb stroked her earlobe, watching as her pupils dilated at his touch. "Give me six months to a year of your time, Trace, and I'll take the kids on. I'm not asking you to renew our wedding vows or even get back together. We just have to…work as partners. For the sake of the kids, until Cleo is fully recovered and we can find a better place for them."

"I don't know. Give me a couple of days to make a decision, okay?"

"You've got it. But as for timeframes, we don't have that long, remember? São João dos Rios has less than a week. And then Cleo—and everyone else—will be escorted out."

CHAPTER FIFTEEN

INSULIN WAS A blessing and a curse.

A blessing because the change in Cleo had been almost immediate when they'd pushed the first dose into her. A curse, because this might be something she'd have to do for the rest of her life.

It explained why her body had taken so much longer to recuperate from the plague than that of her brother. She'd improve a little bit and then go back three steps for seemingly no reason. They'd assumed it was because she was one of the first victims. In reality it had been because the sugar had built up in her system like a toxin, infecting her tissue as surely as the plague had.

The insulin had worked. Today the little girl was well enough to walk the short distance from the village to a clearing to accompany Daniel, Ben and herself as they took care of some important business.

Just like a little family.

And that made her heart ache even more as they caught sight of the first of the cement markers on the other side of a small wooden fence.

"Will I see Mommy again?" Cleo's voice wobbled the tiniest bit.

"I think you will, honey. But only after you've had a long and healthy life."

Tracy wanted to do everything in her power to make sure that happened.

Even move back to *Teresina* for a while?

Ben stopped at an empty site beneath a tree, carrying a flat sandstone rock in one hand and a hammer and chisel he'd found in a neighbor's shed in the other. "How does this spot look?"

"Beautiful," Tracy said. "How about to you guys?"

Cleo nodded, but Daniel remained silent, his mouth set in a mutinous line, looking off to the left. He'd been silent since Cleo had asked if their mother would have a grave and a stone like their grandparents did. But when they'd given the boy a chance to remain behind, he'd trailed along at a distance, before steadily gaining ground until he'd been walking beside Ben.

"*O que foi?*" Cleo went over to Daniel and took his hand in hers, her concern obvious. "*Estás triste?*"

He shook his head. "*Vovô está por aí.*"

Ah, so that's why he was looking in that direction. His grandparents' graves were to the left. Cleo had assumed, like Tracy had, that Daniel was struggling with his grief. And maybe that was partially true. But he also wanted his mom's grave to be next to that of his grandparents.

"Can you show us where they are?" she asked.

Without a word, Daniel trudged to a spot about twenty yards to his left, where a weathered tombstone canted backwards.

Ben laid his tools on the ground and set to righting the stone as best he could, packing dirt into the furrow behind it. The names Louisa and Jorge were inscribed on the top, along with the surname Silva. Louisa had outlived Jorge by fifteen years.

Other than the leaning headstone, the graves were neat, with no weeds anywhere to be seen. They'd been well tended—probably by the mother of Cleo and Daniel. It made it all the more fitting that her grave be next to theirs.

"This is perfect," Tracy said.

Daniel gave a short nod, to which Cleo added her approval.

Kneeling on the packed ground next to her, Ben pulled out the sheet of paper that had the children's mother's full name on it and picked up his chisel and hammer. The first strike rang through the air like a shot, and Cleo flinched. Tracy put her arm around the girl and they stood quietly as the sound was repeated time and time again. A cadence of death…and hope.

Sweat poured down Ben's face and spots of moisture began to appear on his dark T-shirt, but still he continued, letter by letter, until the name of Maria Eugênia da Silva Costa appeared on the stone, along with the dates of her birth and death.

Cleo had stood quietly through the entire process, but when Ben glanced up at her with his brows raised, she knelt beside him. With tender fingers she traced the letters one by one while Daniel stayed where he was. He'd brushed his palm across his face as if chasing away sweat—but Tracy had a feeling a rogue tear or two might have been part of the mix.

Handing a bunch of wildflowers to the little girl, she watched as Cleo and Ben carefully placed the stone and cross, setting the tiny bouquet in front of the objects. Glancing at Ben, who'd slicked his hair back, she cleared her throat. "Would you mind saying a few words?"

Blotting a drizzle of perspiration with his shirt sleeve, he stood, lifting a brow. "It's been a while since I've gone to church."

"I'm sure you can think of something." Tracy knew she'd lose it if she tried to say anything.

Cleo rose as well and gripped her hand fiercely.

"Right." He put his hand on one of Cleo's shoulders and motioned Daniel over. The boy moved forward, his steps unsure as if he didn't want to face the reality of what was about to happen. Tracy knew just how he felt. Somehow seeing your mother's name carved into cold, hard stone made things seem unbearably permanent. Even more permanent than the granite itself.

As if aware of her thoughts, Ben started talking, his voice low and somber. "We want to remember Maria Eugênia and give thanks for her life. For the brave children she brought into this world and nurtured to be such fine, caring individuals." Ben's eyes met hers. "We leave this marker as a reminder of her time on this earth. A symbol that she was important. That she was loved. That she won't be forgotten. By any of us."

Cleo's hands went up to cover her face, her small shoulders shaking in silence, while Daniel stood unmoving. Ben knelt between them. One broad-shouldered man flanked by two grieving children.

Oh, God.

One of the tears she'd been blinking away for the last several minutes threatened to break free. But this was not the time. This wasn't about her. It was about these kids. About helping them through a terrible time in their lives. About helping Cleo get to the root of her medical problems.

She went over and gave Daniel a long hug. And then she knelt in front of Cleo, her eyes meeting Ben's as she brushed a strand of hair from the child's damp head and then dropped a kiss on top of it.

Suddenly she knew she wouldn't need a few days to decide. In the scheme of things, what was six months or a year when she could make a difference in these kids' lives for ever? Wasn't that what she'd come here to do? What she'd done even as she'd faced her test results? As impossibly hard as it might be to see Ben each and every day, she was going to *Teresina*. She was going to help make sure Daniel and Cleo were put in a situation where they could flourish and grow. And where Cleo—as Tracy had promised her—would have that chance at a long and healthy life.

Ben stood in the door of the sickroom and peered around one last time. Every bed was empty of patients, the IV poles disassembled and the military vehicles had headed out one by one, leaving only a small contingent to carry out General Gutierrez's final order. Ben had insisted on staying behind to make sure the last survivors had packed up and moved out of town, which they had.

Maybe it was the life-and-death struggle that had gone on here, maybe it was the unrelenting horror of what they'd seen, but most of the inhabitants had seemed only too happy to clear out. Most of them—except Cleo and Daniel—had relatives to turn to and those who didn't would have help from the government to start over, including jobs and subsidized housing, until they got back on their feet.

Several of the villagers, when they'd discovered what Ben had done for Daniel and Cleo's mother, had made similar monuments for their own loved ones and set them in various locations around the cemetery. Ben had wrung a promise from the general that the graveyard would remain untouched.

São João dos Rios was now a ghost town—already dead to all intents and purposes.

And soon his wife would be moving back into his house with a ready-made family in tow. He wasn't sure what had suddenly caused her to say yes. He only knew as the four of them had knelt in front of Maria Eugênia's grave, she'd met his eyes and given a single nod of her head.

He'd mouthed the words, "You'll go?"

Another slow nod.

There'd been no emotion on her face other than a mixture of grief and determination, and he'd wondered if he'd done the right thing in asking her to come. But he couldn't take on two kids by himself and do them justice. Daniel was a strong young man, a few years from adulthood, and Cleo a young girl whose body was still battling to adapt to diabetes, while her mind buckled under a load of grief and loss.

Right now, Tracy and the kids were going through Daniel and Cleo's house and collecting an assortment of sentimental items, and if he knew Tracy, she was making the case for each and every object with the soldier General Gutierrez had left in charge. His friend wasn't an unreasonable man, but he took his job seriously. He was not going to let this pathogen out of the city, if he could help it.

All clothing and linens had to be boiled before they were packed into crates and given a stamp of approval. The hours had run into days as people waited in line for their turn to sanitize their belongings.

A movement caught his eye and he frowned as he spotted Tracy's assistant heading over to the house. He hadn't realized the man was still here, although in the confusion of the last few hours he couldn't remember seeing him leave. Obviously, he wouldn't have without saying goodbye to his boss.

He turned, ready to follow, when Tracy came out of the house and met him. Pedro said something to her and she shrugged. But when the man laid his hands on her shoulders, a slow tide began to rise in Ben's head and he pushed off to see what was going on.

The first voice to reach his ears was Pedro's. "You can't be serious. *Projeto Vida* is your life. You can't just abandon it. What about the medical ship?"

Tracy shook her head and said something, but he couldn't quite make out her words. Ben moved a little faster.

"Why can't someone else deal with them?"

"Because there is no one else, Pedro. It's something I have to do. You and the rest of the crew can hold the fort until I get back."

Until she got back. Why did those four words make his gut churn?

Pedro evidently saw him coming and took his hands from her shoulders. It didn't stop him from continuing his tirade, though. "How long do you think that will that be?"

"Six months. Maybe a year." She glanced back at the door to the house. "Please, keep your voice down. We haven't talked to the kids about time frames."

"Why don't you just bring the kids down to São Paulo?"

"You know I can't do that. It wouldn't be fair to them or to you all. Our hours are all over the place and we're rarely in the office a week before we're off again."

The turning and shifting in Ben's gut increased in intensity. He hoped that didn't mean she was planning on keeping the same schedule once she got to Teresina. He expected her to be an active partner in Cleo's care, not an absentee parent.

He forced a smile as he addressed Tracy. "Is there a problem?"

She shook her head. "No, we're just working out some details about the office."

That's not what it sounded like to him.

Moistening her lips, she leaned forward to give Pedro a quick hug. "It's going to be all right. Give me a call when you get in. I should have cellphone service once I get on the road."

"Speaking of roads," Ben said, his eyes locked on Pedro, "we should all be heading in that direction. Do you need a ride anywhere?"

"Nope. I offered to help with the clean-up then I'll catch a ride to the airport."

Tracy smiled. "I thought you said the soldiers were 'scary dudes.'"

"They're not so bad once you get to know them. Other people…not so much."

Yeah, Ben could guess who that little jab was meant for. Luckily, his skin had grown pretty thick over the last several years. Not much got through.

Except maybe one hot-tub episode.

And a few hot tears that had splashed on his shoulder as Tracy had confessed her deepest, darkest secret. Oh, yeah, that had gotten through more than he cared to admit.

"I have a crate of embroidered linens that need to be boiled and then we can go."

Pedro, as if finally realizing she was serious about going to *Teresina*, spun on his heel and walked away.

Maybe he should give Tracy one more chance to walk away as well. But as much as he tried to summon up the strength, he couldn't. Not just yet.

He had two kids to worry about.

And maybe someday he could convince himself that was the real reason.

"Where are the beds?"

Ben found Daniel standing in the middle of his new room, the backpack with all his clothes still slung over one of his thin shoulders. At least the boy's cheeks had some color back in them. "It's right there against the wall."

And then he realized why the kid had asked that question. He'd probably never slept on a spring mattress in his life. The military had used canvas cots for sickbeds, while most of the houses in São João dos Rios contained *redes*…hammocks. Ben had nothing against sleeping in them. The things were pretty comfortable, in fact. And making love in one…

Yeah, better not to think about the times he and Tracy had shared one on various trips in their past.

Ben moved past Daniel and sat on the double-sized bed. "This is what we normally sleep on."

"But it's not hanging up. Doesn't it get hot?"

The kid had a point.

"That's why we have fans." He nodded at the ceiling fan that was slowly spinning above them. "It goes at different speeds."

"I don't know…" Daniel looked dubious.

Ben smiled. "Tell you what. Try it for a week or so and if you absolutely hate it, we'll go buy you a *rede*."

"My mom made mine herself. And Cleo's."

His throat tightening, Ben nodded. By now the military would have burned everything. Houses, most material possessions that could carry bacteria out of the city. That included Daniel and Cleo's hammocks. "I know. I wish we could have brought them, but there was no way to boil them."

They'd been able to sterilize a few of Maria Eugênia's aprons and embroidered towels, but hammocks had been too unwieldy. They'd been forced to leave so much behind.

"I understand." He looked around again. "Why is there only one bed, then?"

That was another thing. The siblings had shared a bedroom in their old house, but there were enough rooms here that they wouldn't need to any more. But how to explain that to a boy who'd never had a room of his own. "Cleo will have her own bed, in the room next door to this one."

Tracy was currently in there with the girl, making up the couch with sheets and pillows. He tried to look at his home through their eyes. He wasn't a wealthy man by American standards, but it would certainly seem that way to Cleo and Daniel. There was even an air-conditioner in each of the rooms for when things got unbearably hot.

But he didn't mention that right now. He wanted to give them some time to adjust to their new surroundings before springing too much on them.

The local government had been overwhelmed, dealing with the aftermath of the outbreak, so when Ben had asked permission to take the kids with them, they'd made copies of Ben's and Tracy's identity papers, called in a quick background check, then promised a formal interview in the coming weeks. He knew it would only be a formality. And maybe some long-lost relative would come forward in the meantime and claim the children.

He wasn't sure how he felt about that. In just two weeks Ben had grown fond of the kids. Too fond, in fact.

What had he been thinking, agreeing to this? And what had Tracy been thinking, saying yes?

A question that made something in his chest shimmy to life.

As if she knew he'd been thinking about her, Tracy showed up at the doorway with Cleo in tow. "We're all set up. How are you doing in here?"

Daniel looked up at the sign Rosa had hung on the bedroom wall when Ben had called to tell her the news.

Bem Vindo, Daniel!

There was a matching "welcome home" sign in Cleo's room, with her name on it.

Giving the first tentative smile Ben had witnessed since he'd known the boy, Daniel nodded. "I think we will do very well here."

"So do I."

The soft words came from Tracy, who also had a ghost of a smile on her face. She walked over and took one of his hands, giving it a quick squeeze before releasing it. Then she whispered the two most beautiful words he'd ever heard. "Thank you."

CHAPTER SIXTEEN

"I HAVE A surprise for you outside."

Ben had rounded them all up in the living room.

A surprise—anything, in fact—was better than Tracy trying to avoid looking into the bedroom she'd once shared with Ben. The one that seemed to call to her, no matter where she was in the house.

Tracy glanced at Rosa to see if she knew anything, but she just shrugged.

If the housekeeper was surprised to see Tracy back in *Teresina*, she didn't show it. She'd just engulfed her in a hug so tight it had squeezed the air from her lungs. She'd then dabbed the corners of her eyes with her apron before embracing each of the children.

"A surprise?" asked Cleo. "What is it?"

Giving Ben a puzzled look, Tracy wondered what kind of surprise he could possibly have. They'd only arrived a few hours ago. The kids hadn't even had a chance to explore properly yet.

"I bought a water tank," he said in English. "I thought we could convert it into a makeshift pool for the kids. Maybe even sink it partway into the ground to make it easier to climb into. I had it delivered when you agreed to come to *Teresina*."

Heat suffused her face as she processed this, ignoring the kids who were asking to know what he'd said. "Is it the one from São João dos Rios?" Lord, she hoped not. Those memories were even fresher than the ones from the bedroom down the hall.

"No. Bigger."

"We could have bought an inflatable pool."

"I figured this would be more permanent and less likely to rupture. I can't afford to have a built-in pool put in, but I figured the kids could help with the upkeep. It'll also give them a place to entertain any new friends they might make."

"That was nice, Ben." She refused to wonder what would happen to it once everyone went their separate ways. "I think they'll love it."

Tracy switched back to Portuguese and twitched her index finger back and forth at the kids' expectant glances. "I can't tell you what we said without spoiling the surprise."

Standing aside as Ben pushed the door open, she watched the kids lope into the back yard. A large oval water tank sat in a sandy area. Daniel's eyes touched it then skipped past, still looking for whatever the surprise was.

Ben was right, it was huge. The thing must hold a couple of thousand gallons. Why had they never thought of using one as a pool before? Perched on rooftops everywhere in Brazil, the blue fiberglass tanks came in various shapes and sizes. This one must have been meant for a commercial building.

Cleo seemed just as lost as Daniel was. "Where's the surprise?"

To them, evidently, a *caixa de água* was just that: a holding tank for water. They couldn't see the possibilities.

Ben walked over to it and put his hand on the curved rim. "This is it."

The way both kids' faces fell brought a laugh up from

Tracy's chest. "What? You don't think this is a good surprise?"

Cleo shook her head, and Daniel said, "It's fine. I'm sure you needed a new one."

"Oh, it's not for our roof." Ben motioned them round to the other side of the tank. They followed him, Tracy wondering what he'd hidden over there.

Taped to the outside edge was a glossy magazine ad showing a family playing in an above-ground pool, an inflatable raft bouncing on happy waves.

"This…" Ben patted the side of the tank "…is going to be a pool once we're done with it."

"A *piscina*?" Cleo's voice held a note of awe. "We're going to have a pool?"

"We're going to use the tank as a pool." He ran a hand over the top edge. "You're going to have to help me get it ready. And you'll have to help take care of it once it's set up. But, yes, we're going to have a pool."

"Beleza!" The happy shout came from Daniel, who now walked around the tank with a completely different mindset. "The water will be almost up to my neck."

"Yes, and you'll have to be careful with your sister," Ben said, "because it'll be over her head. I don't want you guys using this without supervision. In fact, I'm going to have a cover installed when it's not in use."

Cleo's fingers trailed over the image of the raft on top of the water.

Catching Ben's grin, Tracy could guess what was coming. "There's a bag on the far side of the tank, Cleo. Why don't you go and look inside?"

The little girl raced around to the other side. They soon heard a squeal. "A float. Just like in the picture. And there are two!"

"One for each of them," Tracy murmured to Ben. "You thought of everything, didn't you?"

"No. Not everything." Something in the words had her gaze swiveling back to him.

"I don't understand."

"I don't imagine you do, but it doesn't matter." He moved away from her before she could really look at him. She heard him talking to the kids then they all came around and walked across the yard behind the house, trying to decide on the best place for the pool. They finally came up with a spot near the *acerola* tree, where they'd at least get some shade during the heat of the day.

As soon as the kids had uncovered all the secrets of the soon-to-be pool, they went off to explore the rest of the backyard, leaving Ben and Tracy alone together.

When her eyes met his, the look was soft and fluid, reminding him of days gone by when he'd brought her flowers unexpectedly or had taken her on a long walk in the park.

Hell, he'd missed that look. Placing his hand out, palm up, he held his breath and waited to see if she'd take it. She did, her cool skin sliding across his. He closed his fingers, his gaze holding hers. "Are you okay with all this?"

"I am."

He'd felt the stab of guilt more than once since she'd agreed to come back with him. Especially after the way they'd parted four years ago.

With a sigh he opened his hand and released her. He'd never really known what she'd been thinking during those last dark days of their marriage. And he wasn't sure he wanted to. Maybe it would just make the rift between them that much deeper.

"I guess I'd better go help Rosa with dinner." She stepped up on tiptoe and gave him a soft kiss. "The kids love their surprise, I can tell. Thank you."

Tracy stood back with a smile, the corners of her eyes

crinkling. Oh, how he loved seeing that. The urge to kiss her came and went without incident. After screwing up so badly in the past, he didn't want to do anything that would send them spinning back to uglier times just when he was beginning to feel he'd made up some ground with her. Maybe with time they'd be able to move past those days and become friends again.

At least that was his hope.

Dr. Crista Morena gently palpated Cleo's abdomen, her brow furrowed in concern. "You know that type-one diabetes can occur at any age." She glanced up at them, and Ben could see the curiosity in her eyes. "You know nothing of her background, her medical history?"

"Just what we observed during the plague outbreak," he said. "Could her pancreas have been affected by the illness?"

She stood and straightened the stethoscope around her neck. "Some cases may be triggered by a viral infection—something in the enterovirus family—that causes an auto-immune response." She helped Cleo sit up. "I want to get some bloodwork done on her, but the finger prick we did when you first came in is right around two-twenty. We'll need to do another with her fasting. I'll send some testers home with you."

Tracy nodded. "Her glucose levels seem to fluctuate for no apparent reason, just like they did while she was sick, so her pancreas must be producing some insulin."

"If it's type one, she could be in the honeymoon phase. You administered insulin to bring her levels back down, right?"

"Yes."

"Doing that can sometimes give the organ a rest, stimulating those last remaining beta cells, which then pump out small quantities of the hormone." She looked at each of them. "If it's type one, the honeymoon phase is only a temporary reprieve. Those cells will eventually stop producing all together."

Ben swallowed. If that was true, Cleo would need constant monitoring for the rest of her life. Temporary would become permanent. He glanced at Tracy to see if she'd come to the same conclusion he had.

Yep. Her hands were clasped tightly in her lap, fingers twisting around each other. Well, taking the kids had been her idea in the first place.

But you agreed.

Besides, it had done him a world of good to hear Cleo's happy laugh when she'd realized what the water tank in the backyard meant. How her eyes had widened when she'd discovered she was getting a room of her own with a new pink bedspread—once the bed they'd ordered for her arrived. He wouldn't trade those moments for anything.

Ben helped Cleo hop off the exam table and motioned to the chair he'd occupied moments earlier. She chose to go to Tracy instead, who opened her arms and hauled the child onto her lap, hugging her close.

His throat tightened further. Tracy looked so right holding a child. Would she have cut back on her traveling if their baby had been born?

If the evidence he'd seen was any indication, the answer to that was no. She'd rushed to São João dos Rios during the outbreak, and Pedro had indicated they'd made quite a few trips during the year.

She saved lives by being in that city.

But at what cost to herself?

None, evidently.

Dr. Morena looked up from Cleo's chart and focused on Tracy. "I understand you practiced pediatric medicine in the past. We could use another doctor here at the clinic. Would you be interested?"

"How did you know that?" She shot him a glance that he couldn't read.

"Ben mentioned you were a doctor when he called to make the appointment."

His heart sped up as he waited to see her reaction. Although his slip had been unintentional, when Dr. Morena had mentioned an opening, he'd wondered if she'd say anything to Tracy.

"I haven't practiced pediatric medicine in quite a few years. I've been dealing more with indigenous tribes so—"

"You treat children in those tribes, don't you?"

"Of course."

Dr. Morena closed the cover of the chart with a soft snap. "It's like riding a bicycle. You never really forget how to deal with those little ones. And you obviously have a knack with them." She nodded at Cleo, who was now snuggled into Tracy's lap. "Give me a call if you're interested."

CHAPTER SEVENTEEN

IT WAS LIKE riding a bicycle.

Dr. Morena's words rang through her head a few days later as she stood in the doorway of her old bedroom.

Being with Ben in that water tank had been like that. Remembered responses and emotions bubbling up to the surface. She ventured a little further into the room, sliding her hand across the bedspread. The same silky beige-striped one they'd had years ago. She was surprised he hadn't bought a new set.

She glanced at the door and then, on impulse, lay across the old mattress and stared up at the ceiling. No one would know. Ben was safely at work right now, and Daniel had taken Cleo to explore the neighborhood. Even Rosa was off shopping for groceries, which meant she had a couple of hours to herself.

She wouldn't stay long, just enough to satisfy her curiosity. She'd passed this room for the last couple of days and had wanted to step inside, but she'd resisted the temptation.

Until now.

So, what does it feel like to lie here?

Just like riding a bicycle.

That thought was both terrifying and exhilarating.

The only thing lacking was Ben. And if he could see her now, he'd probably hit the roof. They'd patched together an uneasy truce since arriving in the city, and she was loath to do anything to rock that particular boat. But the open bedroom door had winked at her, inviting her to step through and relive the past.

Rolling onto her stomach, she grabbed the pillow and buried her face into it, sucking down a deep breath of air.

Yep, Ben still slept on the right side of the bed. His warm masculine scent was imprinted on the soft cotton cover, despite Rosa fluffing the pillows to within an inch of their lives. She'd have to make sure she left things exactly like she'd found them.

Being here felt dangerous…voyeuristic. And incredibly erotic. They'd made love in this bed many, many times. All kinds of positions. Her on top. Him. Her hands trapped above her head. His hands molding her body…making her cry out when the time came.

Just that memory made her tingle, her skin responding to the sudden flurry of images that flashed through her head. Oh, Lord. This was bad.

So bad.

Just like riding a bike.

Sitting on a bicycle was one thing. Putting your feet on the pedals and making them go round and round was another thing entirely.

She knew she should get up. Now. But the temptation to linger and let her imagination run wild—to remember one of their lovemaking sessions—was too great. The one that came to mind was when Tracy had been lying on the bed much like she was now. Only she'd been naked.

Waiting.

The covers pulled down so that Ben would find her just like this when he came home from work.

And he had.

Her nipples drew up tight as she recalled the quiet click of the front door closing. The sound of his indrawn breath as he'd stood in the doorway of this very room and spotted her. Without a word, warm lips had pressed against her neck. Just when she'd started to turn her head, eyelids fluttering open, she'd heard the low command, "Don't look.

She'd obeyed, letting him explore her body and whisper the things he wanted to do to her. His hands had slipped beneath her to cup her breasts, drawing a whimper from her when he'd found the sensitive peaks and gently squeezed.

Even now, Tracy couldn't stop her own hands from replaying the scene, burrowing between her body and the mattress.

"Mmm. Yes."

He'd touched her just like this. Her teeth had dug into her lower lip as she'd let the sensations spiral through her system. Just a hint of friction then more as he'd seemed to sense exactly what she was feeling.

"Ben." The whispered name was low, but in the silence of the house it carried. She let out another puff of breath between pursed lips, even as one hand trailed down her side, her legs opening just a bit.

It wouldn't take long. She was so turned on. Just a minute or two. And she'd relieve the ache that had been growing inside her since their time in the tub. She undid the button on her jeans and her fingers found the juncture at the top of her thighs, sweet, familiar heat rippling through her.

Maybe she should close the door. Just in case. Her head tilted in that direction.

Instead of empty space, her gaze met familiar broad shoulders, which now filled the doorway.

She yanked her hands from beneath her in the space of a nanosecond, molten lava rushing up her neck and scorching her face.

Oh, God! Had he heard her say his name?

"Wh-what are you doing here?"

"I would ask you the same thing, but I think it's fairly

obvious from where I'm standing." He took a step closer, his eyes never leaving hers. And the heat contained in them nearly burned her alive.

The door closed. The lock snicked.

"I was just taking a…" She rolled onto her back and propped herself up on her elbows, realizing her mistake when his gaze trailed to her chest and saw the truth for himself. Even she could feel the desperate press of her nipples against her thin shirt.

He stood at the foot of the bed. "Nap?" He gave her a slow smile. "Must have been having quite some dream, then."

Oh, it was no dream. More like a wish. And Ben had been at the heart of it.

"Wh-why did you just lock the door?" Sick anticipation began strumming through her, even though she already knew the answer.

His hands wrapped around her ankles and hauled her down to the foot of the bed, giving her all the confirmation she needed. "Isn't it obvious, Trace? *I* intend to be the one to finish what you started."

Ben wasn't sure what he'd expected when he'd come home early to spend the weekend with Tracy and the kids, but he certainly hadn't expected to find her in his bed…face buried in his pillow, her hands sliding down her own body.

Then, when she'd said his name, he'd known. She'd been fantasizing about him. About them. About the way they used to be.

He'd gone instantly erect, instantly ready for business. And then she'd turned and looked into his eyes, and he'd seen the fire that had once burned just for him. She still felt it. Just like he did.

It inflamed him. Enticed him.

And he wasn't above taking full advantage of it.

Leaning over the bed and planting his hands on either side of her shoulders, he stared down at her, hungry for the sight of her, hair in gorgeous disarray from being dragged down the bed, her slender body encased in snug jeans and a thin cami top. "Tell me you want me."

She licked her lips. "We shouldn't…"

"Maybe not. But I want to know. Was it me you were imagining?"

"Yes." The airy sigh was all he needed.

He bent down and closed his lips over the nipple he could see so clearly through her shirt, his teeth gripping, loving the tight heat of her against his tongue. She whimpered when he raised his head. "Did you imagine me here?" His knee parted her legs and moved to press tightly against her. "Here?"

Tracy's throat moved as she swallowed. "Yes."

His breath huffed out, and he moved up to whisper in her ear, "Let me, then. We'll sort all the other stuff out later."

She didn't say anything, and he wondered if she might refuse. Then her hands went to the back of his head and pulled him down to her lips, which instantly parted the second their mouths met. He groaned low and long as he accepted the invitation, pushing his tongue inside, tasting, remembering, pressing deep and then withdrawing…only to repeat the act all over again—a mounting heat growing in another part of his body.

Desperation spread through his veins, and he tried to rein in his need, knowing that soon kissing her would no longer be enough. The tiny sound she made in the back of her throat said she felt the exact same way.

This was how it had always been with them. The flames burned higher and faster than either of them wanted, until they were writhing against each other, fighting off the inevitable—knowing it would be over far too soon.

He pulled away, his breath rasping in his lungs. "Take off your shirt," he whispered. "I want to see you."

Tracy's hands went to the bottom of her cami without hesitation and lifted it over her head in a graceful movement that made him want to tear off the rest of her clothing and bury himself deep inside her. But he knew it was better if he didn't touch her for the next couple of minutes.

He nodded at her undergarment. "Bra next."

"Say please."

He swallowed, knowing she was teasing, but at this point he'd say anything she wanted. "Please."

She unclipped the front of the thing and shimmied it off her shoulders, the jiggle of her breasts making his mouth water. God, he wanted her.

He drank in the sight and, just like she always had, she took his breath away. "Touch them. Like you were when I came in." He gave her a wolfish grin as he added, "Please."

Her face turned pink, and this time he wondered if she might leap off the bed and stomp out of the room, but her hands went to her breasts and covered them, her head falling back as she gently massaged them.

This woman got to him like no other ever had. He slid his hand into the tangle of her hair and kissed her long and deep, drinking in everything he could.

He stood again, watching her eyes open and meet his. "Slide your thumbs over your nipples. Slowly. Just like I'm aching to do."

Again she hesitated, but then her hands shifted, the pads of her thumbs skimming over the tight buds in perfect synchrony. She repeated the motion, her gaze never leaving his. "Like this?"

"Oh, exactly like that." His voice had gone slightly hoarse, and he knew no amount of clearing his throat would chase it away. "Don't stop."

Her low moan sent heat skimming down his stomach and beyond.

"Where are the kids?"

"Outside. Rosa's shopping."

"Ah, so that's why you were in here." He stepped between her legs, which were still dangling over the side of the bed. He slowly spread them wider with his stance. "You thought you wouldn't get caught."

"I—I didn't plan it."

"But the second you got on that bed you felt it, didn't you? The things we used to do. Imagined me right here—just like this."

"Ben—"

"Shh. Don't talk. We're alone. We both want this." His fingers moved down to the waistband of her jeans. Her teeth sank into her bottom lip, her hands going completely still. "Uh-uh. I didn't tell you you could stop." He placed his hands over hers and showed her how he wanted her to stroke her breasts.

She moaned again, her hips shifting restlessly on the bed. "I want *you* to do it. Please?"

"Soon." His fingers returned to her jeans and dragged them down her thighs, stepping back so he could tug them the rest of the way off. "I don't want to waste a second of this time."

"The kids—"

"Will find the door locked." He smiled at her. "And you're sleeping. You need your rest."

Her panties were black, just like her lacy bra had been. His hand glided down her sternum, past her bellybutton and stopped, fingers trailing along the line formed by her underwear. He wanted to watch her do that too.

"Tracy." His eyes met hers, and he took her hands in his, running both sets down her stomach until he reached the satin band. "Take them off."

She hooked her thumbs around the elastic and eased them down her hips, over the curve of her butt. When she'd pushed them as far as she could go without sitting up, Ben slid them off the rest of the way.

She was naked. His hands curled around her thighs and pushed them apart, his thumbs caressing the soft inner surfaces, then shifted higher, watching her eyes darken with each excruciating inch he gained. When he reached her center, he found her wet…open. He delved inside, still holding her thighs apart. A low whimper erupted from her throat when he applied pressure to the inner surface, right at the spot she liked best.

Her flesh tightened around his thumb, and she raised her hips stroking herself on him.

"Please, Ben. Now."

He didn't want to. Not yet. But he couldn't hold off much longer. He was already shaking with need.

With one hand he reached for his zipper and yanked it down, freeing himself. They could take it slowly later. Gripping her thighs again, he pulled her closer before filling his hands with her luscious butt and lifting it off the bed. He sank into her, watching as she took him in inch by inch.

Buried inside her, he savored the tight heat, trying his best not to move for several seconds. Tracy had other ideas. She wrapped her legs around him, planting her heels against his lower back and pulled him closer, using the leverage to lift her hips up then let them slide back down, setting up a sensual circular rhythm that wouldn't let up. The result was that, although he held perfectly still, his flesh was gripped by her body, massaged and squeezed and rubbed and…

He gritted his teeth and tried desperately to hold on, but it was no use. Nothing could stop the avalanche once it began.

With a hoarse groan he grabbed her hips and thrust hard into her, riding her wildly, feeling her explode around him with an answering cry even as he emptied himself inside her.

Heart pounding in his chest, he continued to move until there was nothing left and his legs turned to jelly. Slowly lowering her to the bed, he followed her down, pulling her onto her side and gathering her close.

Her breath rasped past his cheek, slowing gradually.

The moment of truth. Was she going to bolt? Or accept what had happened between them?

He took a minute or two to get his bearings then kissed her forehead. "Was it as good as you imagined?"

"Better." Her soft laugh warmed his heart. "Only you had your clothes off in my imagination."

"We'll have to work on that."

"Mmm." She sighed against his throat then licked the moisture that had collected there. "Someone will be coming pretty soon."

"Exactly."

"I meant coming *home*."

Something in Ben's throat tightened at the sound of that word on her tongue. *Home*.

Was that what she considered this place? Or would she take off again the second she had the opportunity?

He'd better tread carefully. Not let himself get too comfortable. Because she considered this a temporary arrangement. And if not for the kids, Tracy wouldn't even be here right now. The fact that she hadn't automatically expected to share his bed spoke volumes. She hadn't planned on returning to their old relationship, no matter how good their little interlude in the water tank had been. Or how much she'd seemed to enjoy their time in this bed.

And she had enjoyed it.

Seeing her pleasuring herself on his bed...*their* bed...

had done a number on his heart. As had her admission of fantasizing about him…not about Pedro or some other faceless man as she'd touched her body.

Yeah. He'd liked that a little too much.

Well, somehow he'd better drag himself back from the edge of insanity and grab hold of reality. Because it wasn't likely Tracy was going to change her mind about staying with him for ever. And, unfortunately, with each day that passed he found that's exactly what he wanted.

CHAPTER EIGHTEEN

TRACY DREW THE insulin into the syringe and gave Cleo a reassuring smile. "You're becoming a pro at these."

This was Cleo's tenth shot, but her glucose levels were still fluctuating all over the place. Whether it was the honeymoon phase that Dr. Morena had mentioned or whether her pancreas would again start pumping out its own supply of insulin was the big question. One no one could seem to answer.

"It still hurts."

"I know. It always will. But sometimes we have to be brave and do what we know is best—even if it hurts."

Like leaving had been four years ago? Because that had hurt more than anything else ever had—that and her miscarriage. Looking back, she knew all kinds of things had led to her flight from *Teresina*. Anger, grief, shock. If Ben hadn't done what he had, she might have stuck it out and tried to make things work. But his actions had been the proverbial last straw…her whole world had collapsed around her, unable to keep functioning under the load she'd placed on it.

And now?

She and Ben hadn't talked about what had happened between them two days ago. There was still a part of her that was mortified that he'd caught her on his bed, but the result had been something beyond her wildest dreams.

He'd been arrogant—and sexy as hell—standing there at the foot of the bed, ordering her to touch herself.

If the front door hadn't clicked open and then shut again, they might have started all over again. But the second the sound had registered, there had been a mad dash of yanking on clothing interspersed with panicked giggles as they'd snuck out of his room to face Rosa and her arm-loads of groceries.

Ben had been a whole lot better at feigning noncha-lance than she had as he'd taken the canvas sacks from the housekeeper and helped her put things away. But the burn-ing glances he'd thrown her from time to time had told her he'd rather be right back in that bed with her.

Heat washed over her as she tried to corral her thoughts and keep them from straying any further down that dan-gerous path.

Tracy rolled up Cleo's shorts. "Ready?"

"I—I think so."

With a quick jab that was designed to cause as little pain as possible, she pushed the needle home and injected the medicine. Other than the quick intake of breath, the little girl didn't make a sound. As soon as Tracy withdrew and capped the syringe, she tossed the instrument into the mini medical waste container they'd set up.

Cleo's voice came from the stool where she was still seated. "Are you going to work for Dr. Morena?"

Ah, so she had heard the doctor as she'd talked to them in the exam room. Tracy didn't have an answer today any more than she'd had one for Ben when he'd asked her much the same question after making love.

They hadn't been together again since that night but he'd gotten into the habit of dropping a kiss on her cheek before he left for work each day. She probably should have moved away the first time he'd done it, but this morning she'd found herself lifting her cheek to him in anticipation.

At this rate, she'd be puckering up and laying one right on his lips very soon.

Probably not a smart idea.

She'd never fooled herself into thinking she didn't love Ben. Of course she did. She'd never stopped. She had been furious with him after the yellow fever incident and had needed time to think about how to deal with everything that had been going on in her life. Only she'd taken too much time, and hiding her condition had become second nature—and had seemed easier than returning to *Teresina* to tell him the truth.

During all those years she'd been gone he'd never called her, never begged her to change her mind. Although she couldn't imagine Ben ever doing that. He was strong, stoic. He'd had to be self-sufficient as a child in order to cope, since his parents had rarely been there for him.

She hadn't been there for him either.

But now he knew why. Didn't that change everything? Wasn't that what those little pecks on the cheek had meant?

She could say she hoped so, but in reality she had no idea. He'd barely had any time to process the information, but how would he feel once he had? She knew she was more than just the sum of her parts, but Ben loved her breasts. That much had been obvious from the heat in his eyes as her hands had cupped them. Stroked over the tips.

And, yep…her mind was right back in the gutter, despite her best efforts.

With a start she realized she was still standing in front of the cabinet, and that Cleo was now frowning up at her with a look of concern. Oh, she'd asked about Dr. Morena and whether she was going to work for her.

"How do you feel about what the doctor said? About me working at the clinic?"

Cleo hopped down from the stool and unrolled the leg

of the shorts. "Does that mean we'll keep on staying with you?"

Afraid to get the girl's hopes up too high, she said, "Why don't you leave the worrying about that to us, okay?" She dropped a quick kiss on her head. "Just know that you are loved."

Ben pushed through the front door, stopping short when the sounds of screaming came from the backyard. Dropping his briefcase on the floor, he yelled for Tracy, but other than those distant shouts his call was met by silence. A sense of weird *déjà vu* settled over him. This was much like the day he'd come home to find Tracy gone.

Except there'd been no shouting that day. Speaking of which…

Moving to the back of the house, he threw open the door that led to the patio. There, in the pool, were three bodies. Only they were very much alive.

In fact, it looked like he'd arrived in the middle of some kind of battle from the looks of the water guns in each person's hands. He walked up the steps to the top of the deck, which was still under construction, and all three pairs of eyes turned to him in a synchronized fashion. Too late, he realized his mistake when Daniel shouted, *"Atire-nele!"*

They all took aim and squeezed their triggers. Water came at him from three different angles, soaking his blue dress shirt and plastering it to his chest. "Hey! Enough already!"

No one listened, but then Tracy, clad in a cherry-red bikini that held his eyes prisoner for several long seconds, ran out of water first. As she was dunking her gun to reload, he pounced, going over the side of the water tank in one smooth move and capturing her gun hand as he hit the water—before she had time to bring it back up. She gave a startled scream when he wrapped his arms around her and took her with him beneath the water. Out of sight of the kids, who were bobbing around him, he planted his lips on Tracy's, a stream of bubbles rising as she laughed against her will. He let her up, where she coughed and spluttered. "Not fair!"

He slicked his hair out of his face, brows lifted. "And shooting me without any warning was?"

"You saw the water guns. We figured that was all the warning you deserved."

Ben stood there, dress shoes lying at the bottom of the pool, obviously ruined by now.

But he wouldn't change this scene for anything in the world. This was what he'd always dreamed of. Except in his daydreams Tracy had stayed by his side for ever. For a minute or two he allowed himself to mourn what might never be. But Tracy was here, right now. And all he wanted to do was pull the loose end on that bikini and see what happened. Only they weren't alone.

But at least she was playing. Laughing at his attempt to kiss her beneath the water. Maybe it was enough for now. He could wait and see how things went. If he didn't get his hopes up too high, they couldn't be dashed. Right?

"So. You planned to ambush me the minute I arrived, did you?"

Daniel gave him another squirt—which hit him squarely in the eye. "Ow!"

Another laugh from Tracy. When was the last time he'd heard her laugh with abandon? Far too long ago.

Her gun was still on the bottom of the pool. Diving beneath the water, he retrieved it and came back up, his head just barely above the surface as he let water fill the reservoir. Then he went on the attack, giving back as good as he got. Tracy stayed well out of the line of fire this time, double checking her bikini to make sure she was still in it. The act distracted him for a second and both the kids got him again.

He glared at his wife, mimicking her earlier words. "Not fair."

"Oh, but you know what they say. All's fair in…" Her voice trailed away, her smile dying with it.

He cursed himself, even though he knew it wasn't his fault. Instead, he waved the kids off for a minute and jogged over to her. Draping an arm around her waist, he whispered in her ear. "Let's just take it a day at a time, okay? No expectations."

The smile she gave him was tremulous. "I feel awful, Ben."

"Don't." He kissed her cheek. "Although I think you owe me a new pair of shoes."

"Done." She slid back beneath the water and leaned against the side. "This was a great idea. The kids love it. I'm thinking of enrolling Cleo in swimming lessons. Did you know she doesn't swim?"

Tracy had switched to English so the kids wouldn't understand her. He glanced at Cleo, who was hanging onto the side of the tank with one hand while maneuvering the water gun with the other. He answered her back in the same language. "She definitely needs to learn if the pool is going to stay up year round. How about Daniel?"

"He had lessons in school, but he's never had a place to practice. So it might not be a bad idea for him to brush up on his skills as well."

"Right." He leaned back beside her, stretching his legs out beneath the water. Tracy's limbs looked pale next to the black fabric of his slacks. "Did you put sunscreen on?"

"SPF sixty. The kids have some on as well."

He touched her nose, which, despite her sun protection, was slightly pink. "How long have you guys been in the water?"

"About an hour. We were making a list of recipes that the kids' mother used to fix, and I felt like we needed to do something fun afterwards. I don't want every memory of their mom to end on a sad note."

"Smart." Ben paused, wondering how to ask the question that had been bothering him for the last couple of days. His timing tended to suck, so why worry about that now? "Listen, I've been meaning to ask. About the other night…"

She tensed beside him. "I don't think now is the best time to talk about this."

"I haven't exactly been able to get you alone." Whether that had been on purpose or not, only Tracy could say. "I'll say it in English, so no one else will understand. Are you okay?"

"Okay?"

"Are you upset with me for the way I…?"

He didn't know how else to ask it. And he wasn't sure if he was asking if Tracy was okay, or if "they" were okay.

She shook her head, eyes softening. "No. Of course I'm not upset."

"You've been acting a little funny."

"This whole situation is a little funny." She sighed. "I never expected to be back in *Teresina*."

"Are you sorry you came?"

Ben wasn't sure why he was pushing so hard for reassurance, but he felt like he was slipping and sliding around, searching for something that might or might not be there.

"No. But I was going to tell you something later today. I made a phone call and talked to my old doctor here. She got me an appointment with a surgeon on Monday."

He froze, then a million and one questions immediately came to mind. She gave a quick nod at the kids, who, Ben realized, were both looking at them, trying to figure out what was being said. "Okay. Let's discuss it after dinner, okay?"

"Thank you." She switched back to Portuguese. "Is the military still monitoring your movements?"

He'd mentioned an unmarked vehicle parked in the lot at the hospital since they'd gotten back to *Teresina*. He hadn't recognized it and the driver was always the same person. It was either the military or a terrorist, Ben had told her with a rueful smile. The latter wasn't very likely in Brazil, since it was a pacifist country.

"The car hasn't been in the lot for the last two days so hopefully, if it was the General's doing, they've decided I'm too boring to keep tabs on." He pulled a face at the kids.

Tracy laughed. "Those guys don't know you very well, then, do they, Dr. Almeida? You're quite unpredictable."

The way she said it warmed his heart, despite the chill he'd felt when she'd mentioned the word "surgeon."

He planted a hand on his chest as if wounded and winked at Cleo. "You think I'm a pretty boring guy, don't you?"

The little girl giggled then shook her head.

"What about you?" he asked Daniel.

The boy scratched his head with the tip of his water gun. "I guess you're okay. Not too boring."

Tracy grinned then shot Ben a smug look. "See? Told you."

They were throwing playful barbs at each other again. His spine relaxed. How good it felt to be back on solid footing, instead of crashing around in a scary place where you couldn't see the bottom for the muck.

At least for today. Monday might bring something altogether different.

Ben had knocked on her door that night around midnight. She'd been half expecting him to come and see her out of earshot of the kids. What she hadn't expected was for him to push the door shut with his foot and stand there, staring at her.

Then he'd swept her in his arms and kissed her as if there was no tomorrow. They'd made love on her bed, and it had been as fresh and new as the other two times they'd been together. Afterwards, he'd held her in his arms.

"Whatever happens on Monday, we'll face it together, okay?"

A little sliver of doubt went through her chest. "Are you saying you want to go with me?"

"Would that be okay?"

Tracy had to decide to let him in completely or shut him out. "What about your work?"

"I can take off for a couple of hours." Ben caught a strand of her hair, rubbing it between his fingertips.

"Okay." Whew. Why did that feel so huge? "I won't make any firm decisions until Cleo's diabetes is under control, but I just need to see where I am. I've been neglecting my tests and want to get caught up with them."

"Why now?"

"I don't know. Maybe I've been running away from making a decision one way or the other."

He nodded and wrapped the lock of hair around his finger. "If I asked you to start sleeping in our old bed again, would you say yes?"

"Tonight? Or...?"

"Not just tonight. From now on."

Wow. This had gone from talking about her appointment to Ben asking her to make their marriage a real one. At least that's what she thought he was asking. "I assume by sleeping, you don't actually mean closing our eyes."

The right side of his mouth quirked up. "I definitely think there might be some eye closing going on, but it would take place well before any actual sleeping."

Tracy's body quickened despite having just made love

with this man fifteen minutes ago. She tilted her head as if in deep thought. "Hmm. I don't know. Do you snore?"

"Interesting question. I do make sounds from time to time, but I don't know if I'd call them snoring." His fingers tunneled into her hair, massaging her head in tiny circles that made her shiver.

"I think I remember those sounds. I kind of liked them."

"Did you, now?" His thumb trailed down the side of her throat, stroking the spot where her pulse was beginning to pick up speed in response to his words and his touch.

"Mmm."

He leaned over and kissed the side of her jaw. "And I kind of like the little sound you just made."

"I'm glad, because if you keep that up, I'm going to be making a lot more of— Oh!" Her breath caught as his teeth nipped the crook of her neck, sucking the blood to the surface and then licking over it with his warm tongue.

"Say yes," he whispered.

"Yes." She wasn't sure what she was agreeing to, but it didn't really matter at this point. She wasn't about to hold anything back, and she trusted him enough to know he wouldn't ask her for more than she could give.

He moved to her lips. "Yes to sleeping in my bed?"

"I thought we'd already decided that."

"No, you were still questioning whether or not I snored." His tongue slowly licked across her mouth.

"No snoring. Just sounds." As she said each word, his tongue delved into her mouth before finally cutting off her speech altogether.

I didn't matter, though, because Tracy was already beyond rational thought, her arms winding around his neck.

She was ready to lose herself to him all over again—for as long as he wanted her.

CHAPTER NINETEEN

BEN WAS STILL groggy with sleep when he reached across the bed and realized Tracy was no longer there. He could hear her talking softly from somewhere nearby, and he woke up the rest of the way in a flash.

"But I have a doctor's appointment on Monday." There was a pause. "I suppose I could. It's not urgent."

Ben sat up in bed, looking for her. She must be in the bathroom.

He wasn't purposely trying to eavesdrop, but something about the way she kept her voice hushed said she wasn't anxious for anyone to hear the conversation.

"I don't want to be gone long. Cleo's still getting her shots regulated."

Climbing out of bed and reaching for his boxers, he padded to the door. "Pedro, I can't leave right this second. No, I know. I'm sure Rosa won't mind watching them while Ben is at work. She used to watch him when his parents were gone. I'd have to teach her how to give Cleo her insulin shots, though."

Rosa won't mind watching them.

The soft warmth he'd felt during the night evaporated. Why would Rosa need to watch the kids? Or give Cleo her shots?

Unless Tracy was planning to be gone for a while.

And why was she talking to Pedro in the bathroom, unless she was keeping something from him?

It wouldn't be the first time.

They'd been home less than a week, and she was already off somewhere?

A jumble of emotions spun up inside him like a tornado, anger being the first to reach the top.

No. He was not heading down this path again. He turned the knob and pushed the door open.

Tracy's mouth rounded in a perfect "O" that had looked incredibly sexy last night. But all he saw this morning was betrayal.

"Pedro, hold on just a second."

She put her hand over the phone, but Ben beat her to the punch. "You're leaving."

Licking her lips, she nodded. "Just for a few days. The medical boat docked at a flooded village. There are five cases of cholera and there's certain to be dozens more, as they've all been drinking from the same water source."

"Send someone else." His voice was cold and hard, but that's how he felt inside. "Let Pedro deal with it."

"He's not a doctor, Ben. I am. Matt called him, they're expecting to be overwhelmed by—"

"You're *a* doctor. Not the only doctor in the whole country. You have responsibilities here."

"Rosa can—"

Fury washed over him. "Rosa practically raised my brother and me. These kids need a steady presence in their lives, not be pushed off on someone else every time your assistant has a runny nose. You promised me at least six months."

"It's only this one time."

He closed his eyes for a second, his hand squeezing the doorknob for all he was worth. Then he took a deep breath. "I'm going to lay it out for you, Tracy. Either you let someone else handle this, and we start looking toward a future. Together. Or I'm filing for divorce. Even if I have to go all the way to New York to do it."

Every ounce of color drained from her face. "Wh-what about Daniel and Cleo? You said you couldn't do this alone."

"It doesn't look like I have much of a choice." He shot her a glance. "*I* made a promise that I intend to keep. Besides, I've been through the same rinse-and-spin cycle a couple of times already. I'm sure I can figure things out."

Just before he pulled the door shut he added, "Finish your conversation, then let me know what you decide."

Tracy draped a moist cloth over the forehead of the woman she was treating then used a gloved hand to check her vitals. They were through the worst of the cholera outbreak. There were several army doctors among their group, but this time they hadn't been sent at the request of her husband but were instead digging drain fields and latrines in an effort to prevent a recurrence.

Ben wouldn't send anyone for her this time, because he was through with her. He'd said as much.

She wasn't sure why Pedro's call had spurred her to action. Maybe her instincts were programmed to bolt at the first sign of trouble.

Like having an actual appointment with a doctor? Was she still running...still having to move and work to feel alive?

No, she'd felt alive with Ben as well. And this trip felt hollow. It didn't fulfill her the way it might have a few years ago. She missed the kids. Missed Ben.

Matt's wife sat down beside her on an intricately woven mat. "How are you holding up?"

Stevie had been with *Projeto Vida* for two years, working alongside her husband. They had a daughter as well, but she was confined to the boat this trip. Neither Matt nor Stevie wanted to run the risk of her becoming ill.

"As well as anyone."

Stevie gave her a keen look. "Are you sure about that?"

"We're all tired. I came here to help."

"And you have." Stevie touched her gloved hand to Tracy's. "How's Ben?"

She flashed the other woman a startled look. Word evidently traveled fast. "I wouldn't know. I won't be heading back there."

"I'm sorry."

"Me too." She gave her patient's shoulder a gentle squeeze and murmured that someone would check on her in just a little while then she stood with a sigh. "How do you do it?"

Stevie got to her feet as well. "What do you mean?"

"How do you keep your marriage together and travel on the boat?"

"We both believe in what we do." She stripped her gloves off and motioned for Tracy to follow her. Once outside the tent she leaned against a tree. "Sometimes I just need a breath of fresh air, you know?"

Tracy did know. The smells of illness got to you after a while.

Letting her head bump the bark of the tree trunk, Stevie swiveled her head toward her. "Matt wasn't sure he wanted to come back to Brazil after losing so much here. If he'd chosen to stay in the States, I would have stayed with him. Because that's the only important thing—that we're together."

"So you're saying I shouldn't have come."

"No." Stevie gave her a soft smile. "Only you know what's right…what's in your heart."

"I don't know any more. Ben never liked me traveling."

"I'm sure he missed you very much when you were gone."

"Yes, I suppose he did. But other wives travel."

"As much as you do?" Stevie paused for a moment or two. "I think you have to examine your heart and decide what it is you want out of life. Why you're so driven to do what you do."

Because she didn't have to think about anything else when she was helping people?

In the past she'd worked herself to exhaustion day after day—had fallen into bed at night, her eyes closing as soon as her head had hit the pillow.

Movement equaled life.

But was this really living? Was she doing this because she believed in her work or because she was afraid to stay in one place, where she might start feeling trapped— claustrophobic?

She'd missed her doctor's appointment to be here. Could she not have delayed her flight for a few hours? In reality, despite Pedro's dire predictions, there'd been enough hands to fight the cholera outbreak, even if she hadn't been here. She'd been living her whole life as if she were single with no commitments. Yes, she'd had this job before she'd met Ben. But in choosing it over him time and time again she'd been sending the message that he meant no more to her than he'd meant to his parents.

Lord, she'd made such a mess of things. Such a mess of her life.

And in staying so incredibly busy, she'd not only risked her long-term health but she'd also lost sight of the person she loved most: Ben.

Maybe it was time to start pulling away. Let someone else take the helm of her organization—Pedro maybe— and go back to practicing medicine in a clinic. She might not be able to help whole swaths of people but she could help them one at a time.

Which path was more valuable in the long run? Maybe it wasn't a question of either/or. Maybe each had its own place in the grand scheme of things. And there were two children who'd trusted her to be there for them.

She turned and hugged her friend. "Thank you. I think I've just realized where I should be."

"In *Teresina*?"

She nodded. "I don't know why I didn't see it before now."

"Maybe because 'now' was when you needed to see it." With a secretive smile Stevie waved to her husband, who was working off in the distance. He winked back.

And Tracy did what she should have done four years ago: she walked to the nearest soldier and asked if she could hitch a ride on the next boat out of the Amazon.

Ben sucked down a mouthful of tepid coffee and grimaced before going back to his microscope and glaring down at the slide beneath the lens. He had no business being here today. He'd had no business here all week.

Why had he drawn that ridiculous line in the sand and dared her to cross it? Maybe because he'd never forgiven his parents for withholding their affection when he'd been a child?

Yeah, well, he was an adult now. Well past the age of holding grudges.

He hadn't heard from Tracy since she'd left, and he'd cursed himself repeatedly for not being more sensitive the last time they'd talked…for not trying to really listen to what she'd been saying.

He wasn't the only one who was upset.

Rosa had chewed his butt up one side and down the other when she'd found out Tracy wasn't coming home.

"I used to think I raised you to be a smart boy, Benjamin Almeida. Now I'm not so sure."

"You shouldn't have had to raise me at all."

"Was it so bad? Your childhood?"

He thought back. No, his parents had been gone for months at a time, but when they had been there there'd been laughter…and then, when they'd left again there'd been tears. But through it all Rosa had been there. How many children grew up not even having a Rosa in their lives?

If he thought about it, he was damned lucky.

And if he'd given Tracy a little more time to settle in before jumping to conclusions at the first phone call she'd got from the office, maybe he could have done a better job at being a husband this time.

He rummaged around in his desk until he came up with an old tattered business card that he'd saved for years. Staring at the familiar name on the front, he turned it over and over between his fingers, battling with indecision. He knew from their time in São João dos Rios that the phone number was still the same. Finally, before he could change his mind, he dialed and swiveled around in his chair to face out the window.

Did she even have cellphone reception wherever she was?

He heard the phone ring through the handset, but there was something weird about it. Almost as if it was ringing in two places at once—inside his ear and somewhere off in the distance. On the second ring the sound outside his ear grew louder in steady increments, and he frowned, trying to figure out if he was just imagining it. On the third ring her voice came through. "Hello?"

Ben's breath seized in his lungs as he realized the greeting came not only from the handset pressed to his ear but from right behind him. He slowly swiveled and met sea-green eyes. They crinkled at the corners as they looked back at him.

Keeping the phone pressed to his ear, he gazed at her in disbelief, while she kept her phone against her own ear as well.

"Tracy?"

"Yes."

God, he could just jump up and crush her to him. But he didn't. He said the words he'd been rehearsing for the last half-hour. "I've missed you. Please come home."

Tears shimmered in her eyes, her throat moving in a quick jerking motion. "I've missed you too. I'll be there soon."

With that she clicked her phone shut and moved towards him. When she stood before his chair, he reached up and pulled her down onto his lap. "You're home."

"I am. I'm home." She wrapped her arms around his neck and pulled him against her. "And this time I'm here to stay."

One year later

Ben strode down the hallway of Einstein Hospital in São Paulo, Brazil, until he reached the surgical wing. Tracy's dad was already in the waiting room. He stood as he saw Ben heading his way. The two men shook hands, Sam taking it one step further and embracing his son-in-law.

Ben said, "I'm glad you were able to come, sir."

"How is she?"

"Still in surgery."

The months since Tracy had stood in his office and they'd shared declarations of love had passed in a flurry of medical tests for both Cleo and Tracy. Cleo's initial diagnosis of diabetes had been confirmed, but it was now under control. They'd even been granted custody of both children.

Tracy's mammogram had come back with an area of concern and whether it was cancer or not, they both knew it was time. They'd made this decision together soon after she'd come home. She'd shed tears while Ben had reassured her that he'd love her with breasts or without.

Nodding to the chair Sam had vacated, they both sat down.

"She did it, then," his father-in-law said.

"Yes." Ben leaned forward, elbows on his knees, clasped hands dangling between them. "She wanted to be proactive."

Tracy's dad nodded. "If her mother had known she carried this gene, I know in my heart she would have done the same thing. And I would have stood beside her." He dragged a forearm across his eyes, which Ben pretended he didn't see. "How long will she be back there?"

"Two to four hours." He glanced at his watch. "It's going on three hours now. We should be hearing something fairly soon."

Two to four hours. Such a short time. And yet it seemed like for ever.

Unable to sit still, he settled for pacing while Sam remained in his seat. Ben had already made all kinds of deals with God, so many he wasn't sure he'd be able to keep track. But Tracy had been so sure of this, so at peace with her decision in the past week.

A green-suited man came around the corner, a surgical mask dangling around his neck. "Mr. Almeida?"

Ben moved towards him, Sam following close behind. The surgeon frowned, but Ben nodded. "This is Tracy's dad. He's just arrived in town."

The man nodded. "The surgery went fine. I didn't see

any definite areas of malignancy, but I'm sending everything off to pathology for testing just in case."

"Tracy's okay, then?" Ben didn't want to hear about malignancies or what they had or hadn't found.

"She's fine." The man hesitated. "Reconstruction shouldn't be a problem. We'd like to keep her here for a day or two to observe her, however. Will she have someone to help her at home afterwards?"

"Yes." Ben's and Sam's answers came on top of the other, causing all of them to smile.

Ben finished. "We'll make sure she gets everything she needs." He knew the kids would both be beside themselves, desperate for a chance to talk to Tracy. But he'd left them in *Teresina*, in Rosa's care—though he'd realized the irony of it. Kids survived. And these two kids had survived more than most…more than he'd ever had to, even on his worst days.

"Good," the surgeon said. "Give us a few minutes to get her settled then someone will come and get you. Please, don't stay long, though. She needs to rest."

Ben held out a hand. "Thank you. For everything."

The surgeon nodded then shook each of their hands and headed back in the direction from which he'd come. Before he rounded the corner, though, he turned and came back. "I wanted to tell you what a brave young woman Tracy is. I don't know how much you've talked about everything, but whether you agree with her decision or not it was ultimately up to her. Support her in it."

"Absolutely." Ben wasn't planning on doing anything else. He'd spend the rest of his days supporting whatever decisions she made. He was just grateful to have her back.

"Thanks again."

"You're welcome. Take care." This time the surgeon didn't look back but disappeared around the corner.

"Why don't you go back and see her first?" Ben told Sam.

"My face is not the one she'll want to see when she wakes up. There's plenty of time."

Yes, there was. Ben swallowed. "Thank you. I'll tell her you're here."

Sleep.

That's all Tracy wanted to do, but something warm curled around her hand and gave a soft squeeze. Someone said her name in a low, gravelly voice she should recognize.

Did recognize.

"Trace."

There it was again. Her heart warmed despite the long shivers taking hold of her body. She was cold. Freezing. Her body fought back, shuddering against the sensation.

Something settled over her. A blanket?

She focused on her eyelids, trying to convince them to part—wanted to put a hand to her chest to see if they were still there.

Oh, God. Moisture flared behind still closed lids and leaked out the sides.

"Tracy." Warm fingers threaded through her own. "You're okay. Safe. I'm here."

She wanted to believe. But she was afraid the last year had all been a dream. At least the blanket was starting to warm her just a bit.

Her throat ached. From the tube she'd had down her throat.

Wait. Tube?

Yes, from the surgery. Ben was here. Somewhere. He promised to be here when she woke up.

So why was she even doubting she'd heard his voice?

Okay. Moment of truth.

Eyelids...open.

As if by magic, they parted and the first thing she saw

was the face. The gorgeous face that matched that low, sexy voice. Broad shoulders stretched wide against the fabric of his shirt. Ruffled brown hair that looked like he'd shoved fingers through it repeatedly, a piece in the back sticking straight up.

Long, dark lashes. Strong throat. Gentle hands.

Her husband.

"Ben?" The sound rasped out of her throat as if coated by rough sandpaper—and feeling like it as well.

"I'm here."

Yes, it was Ben. He was here. Crying?

Oh, God. He was crying because she no longer had breasts. No, that wasn't it. They'd made this decision together. Had they found something during the surgery?

She tried to glance down at herself, but everything was buried under a thick layer of blankets. But there was no pain. Could the surgeon not have taken them?

"Are they…?"

"Shh. You're fine."

Closing her eyes, she tried to clear her fuzzy head. "The kids?"

"I spoke to Rosa a few minutes ago. They're fine. They miss you."

I miss you.

Her lips curved as she remembered Ben saying those very words as she'd stood in the doorway of his office a year ago. That he'd actually called her—wanted her to come home—was a memory she'd treasure for ever.

Where was the pain? Shouldn't it hurt to have something sliced off your body?

"I miss the kids, too."

He smiled and smoothed strands of hair back from her face. "Your dad's here. They'll only let one of us in at a time, and he insisted you'd want to see me first."

"He was right."

Lifting her hand to his lips, he kissed the top of it. His touch was as warm as his voice. "I love you, Tracy. And I'm going to spend the rest of my life showing you how much."

She closed her eyes, only to have to force them open again. "I like the sound of that."

One of the nurses appeared in the doorway, leaning against the frame. "We probably need to let Mrs. Almeida get some sleep."

"Mrs. Almeida." Tracy murmured the words as her eyelids once again began to flicker shut. She loved having his name.

Almost as much as she loved the man who'd given it to her.

EPILOGUE

THE SUNRISE WAS gorgeous, a blazing red ball of fire tossed just above the horizon by the hand of God.

Today promised to be a scorcher—just like most days in *Teresina*. And she relished each and every one of them. Curling her hands around the railing of the deck off their bedroom, Tracy let the warmth of the wood sink into her palms and gave a quiet sigh of contentment. She loved these kinds of mornings.

Five years since her surgery and no sign of cancer.

Tracy was thrilled to be a part of Crista Morena's thriving pediatric practice. And twice a year she and Ben took a trip along the Amazon to do relief work. Together. Something that might have been impossible in the past.

A pair of arms wrapped around her from behind, sliding beneath the hem of her white camisole and tickling the skin of her tummy. She made a quiet sound, putting her hands over his and holding him close. Leaning her head against her husband's chest, she thought about how truly blessed she was.

Except for one thing.

"I miss Daniel." The wistfulness in her heart came through in her voice.

Their adopted son had left for college in the States last month and was busy studying to be a doctor—hoping to return to Brazil and help people in communities like São

João dos Rios. His mother would be so very proud of the man her son had become. The four of them had made several trips back to the kids' home town, and although the razed village was sad testament to what had happened there, it was also a place of joy. A place of new beginnings.

They'd had a permanent stone marker made and had placed it on Maria Eugênia's grave—although both Daniel and Cleo had decided the crude rock Ben had carved should remain there as well.

They'd also made a pact to go back once a year to put flowers on her grave.

Cleo, now thirteen, was growing into a beautiful young woman who was sensitive and wise beyond her years. All too soon she'd be grown as well, leaving them to start a life of her own.

"We can always phone Daniel later this afternoon." Ben planted cool lips on her neck.

"We'll wait for Cleo to get home from school. I can't believe how fast time has gone by."

"I'm grateful for every moment." His lips continued to glide up her neck until he reached her earlobe, biting gently.

She shivered, her body reacting instantly, the way it always did for this man. "So am I."

A thin cry came from the back of the house. Tracy squinched her nose and sighed. "So is someone else."

Their baby girl, just three months old, was letting them know she was hungry. Although she would never replace the baby they'd lost all those years ago, trying to have another child had seemed the right thing to do. Tracy was grateful for second chances, no matter how they came.

Ben had taken a little more coaxing—a year to be exact. He'd been worried about the ramifications to her health, but in the end he'd agreed. And Grace Elizabeth Almeida had come into the world kicking and screaming.

Someone ready to take on the universe and everything it held.

"I guess we'd better go feed her before she gets really wound up." Ben turned her in his arms and nipped her lower lip. "Although I was hoping we might get a little alone time. Just this once."

"Don't worry, Ben. We have plenty of time. Our whole lives, in fact."

Tracy sighed, her happiness complete. She had everything she could possibly want out of life. She and Ben had found their middle ground, despite seemingly impossible odds. And she'd discovered there was more than one path to happiness, as long as the man she loved was by her side. And as her three children had taught her, there was definitely more than one way to make a family.

* * * * *

Mills & Boon® Hardback

January 2014

ROMANCE

The Dimitrakos Proposition	Lynne Graham
His Temporary Mistress	Cathy Williams
A Man Without Mercy	Miranda Lee
The Flaw in His Diamond	Susan Stephens
Forged in the Desert Heat	Maisey Yates
The Tycoon's Delicious Distraction	Maggie Cox
A Deal with Benefits	Susanna Carr
The Most Expensive Lie of All	Michelle Conder
The Dance Off	Ally Blake
Confessions of a Bad Bridesmaid	Jennifer Rae
The Greek's Tiny Miracle	Rebecca Winters
The Man Behind the Mask	Barbara Wallace
English Girl in New York	Scarlet Wilson
The Final Falcon Says I Do	Lucy Gordon
Mr (Not Quite) Perfect	Jessica Hart
After the Party	Jackie Braun
Her Hard to Resist Husband	Tina Beckett
Mr Right All Along	Jennifer Taylor

MEDICAL

The Rebel Doc Who Stole Her Heart	Susan Carlisle
From Duty to Daddy	Sue MacKay
Changed by His Son's Smile	Robin Gianna
Her Miracle Twins	Margaret Barker

ROMANCE

Challenging Dante	Lynne Graham
Captivated by Her Innocence	Kim Lawrence
Lost to the Desert Warrior	Sarah Morgan
His Unexpected Legacy	Chantelle Shaw
Never Say No to a Caffarelli	Melanie Milburne
His Ring Is Not Enough	Maisey Yates
A Reputation to Uphold	Victoria Parker
Bound by a Baby	Kate Hardy
In the Line of Duty	Ami Weaver
Patchwork Family in the Outback	Soraya Lane
The Rebound Guy	Fiona Harper

HISTORICAL

Mistress at Midnight	Sophia James
The Runaway Countess	Amanda McCabe
In the Commodore's Hands	Mary Nichols
Promised to the Crusader	Anne Herries
Beauty and the Baron	Deborah Hale

MEDICAL

Dr Dark and Far-Too Delicious	Carol Marinelli
Secrets of a Career Girl	Carol Marinelli
The Gift of a Child	Sue MacKay
How to Resist a Heartbreaker	Louisa George
A Date with the Ice Princess	Kate Hardy
The Rebel Who Loved Her	Jennifer Taylor

Mills & Boon® Hardback

February 2014

ROMANCE

A Bargain with the Enemy	Carole Mortimer
A Secret Until Now	Kim Lawrence
Shamed in the Sands	Sharon Kendrick
Seduction Never Lies	Sara Craven
When Falcone's World Stops Turning	Abby Green
Securing the Greek's Legacy	Julia James
An Exquisite Challenge	Jennifer Hayward
A Debt Paid in Passion	Dani Collins
The Last Guy She Should Call	Joss Wood
No Time Like Mardi Gras	Kimberly Lang
Daring to Trust the Boss	Susan Meier
Rescued by the Millionaire	Cara Colter
Heiress on the Run	Sophie Pembroke
The Summer They Never Forgot	Kandy Shepherd
Trouble On Her Doorstep	Nina Harrington
Romance For Cynics	Nicola Marsh
Melting the Ice Queen's Heart	Amy Ruttan
Resisting Her Ex's Touch	Amber McKenzie

MEDICAL

Tempted by Dr Morales	Carol Marinelli
The Accidental Romeo	Carol Marinelli
The Honourable Army Doc	Emily Forbes
A Doctor to Remember	Joanna Neil

Mills & Boon® Large Print
February 2014

ROMANCE

The Greek's Marriage Bargain	Sharon Kendrick
An Enticing Debt to Pay	Annie West
The Playboy of Puerto Banús	Carol Marinelli
Marriage Made of Secrets	Maya Blake
Never Underestimate a Caffarelli	Melanie Milburne
The Divorce Party	Jennifer Hayward
A Hint of Scandal	Tara Pammi
Single Dad's Christmas Miracle	Susan Meier
Snowbound with the Soldier	Jennifer Faye
The Redemption of Rico D'Angelo	Michelle Douglas
Blame It on the Champagne	Nina Harrington

HISTORICAL

A Date with Dishonour	Mary Brendan
The Master of Stonegrave Hall	Helen Dickson
Engagement of Convenience	Georgie Lee
Defiant in the Viking's Bed	Joanna Fulford
The Adventurer's Bride	June Francis

MEDICAL

Miracle on Kaimotu Island	Marion Lennox
Always the Hero	Alison Roberts
The Maverick Doctor and Miss Prim	Scarlet Wilson
About That Night...	Scarlet Wilson
Daring to Date Dr Celebrity	Emily Forbes
Resisting the New Doc In Town	Lucy Clark